SEX LIES & VAMPIRE HUNTERS

NIGHT SHIFT SERIES BOOK #1

MYLA JACKSON

TWISTED PAGE INC

EBOOK ISBN: 978-1-62695-136-5

PRINT ISBN: 978-1-62695-135-8

SEX, LIES & VAMPIRE HUNTERS

NIGHT SHIFT SERIES BOOK #1

Award Winning Author
Myla Jackson

Julie Taylor tipped the vial upside down and jammed the syringe into the rubber covering. Just two more hours and she could go home and get off her aching feet. When she had the desired dose, she removed the needle and set the glass vial on the cart.

"Don't look now, but guess who just pulled up in his squad car?" a gravelly, feminine voice whispered into her ear.

The bottle slipped from her suddenly nerveless fingers and would have crashed to the floor if she hadn't slammed her hip against the cart, catching it between the cart and her scrubs. Whew! "Kim Erickson, don't do that!"

Kim giggled and sashayed out of reach. "Thought you'd want to know. But if you don't care..." Her eyebrows rose questioningly. "I'll tell him you're not interested." The flirty behavior was a marked contrast to Kim's long bottle-black hair and Goth makeup. Kim was a dichotomy of sweet and weird wrapped up in a slightly plump package. Despite Kim's strange appearance, Julie couldn't find a better friend.

"Don't you dare!" Syringe in hand, Julie followed Kim out into the hallway.

"Hey! Watch it with that thing," Dorothy Lindeman, or Dottie, the battle-axe, head nurse of the nightshift, dodged around her pointed needle. "Get that medication into the patient in Room 1 before you stick someone else with it." Battle-axe in spirit only, Dorothy was anything but large and ugly. However, she could be mean when you didn't do as she said.

Julie hurried toward Room 1 where Mrs. Thompson struggled to breathe through a severe asthma attack. All the while she ministered to her patient, her thoughts were on the gorgeous cop who'd chosen to target her with his flirting ways. Damn, she was lucky. Roger Decker was the sexiest hunk this side of the Mississippi and he wanted her.

Julie sighed. If only they could get their shifts synchronized so they could spend time together.

Mrs. Thompson was resting easily, her breathing returning to normal.

Julie slipped out into the hallway and turned toward the nurses station for her next assignment. Before she could take two steps, her friend Kim snagged her by the elbow and marched her toward the supply closet. "What? Where are you taking me?"

"Shut up. You'll thank me later." Kim opened the closet door and shoved her inside, closing the door behind her.

The closet was dark and filled with the acrid scent of disinfectant floor cleaners and old mops. Julie fumbled in the dark for the doorknob. When she found it, she twisted the handle and pulled. It didn't budge. "What's the deal?"

"I'm the deal." A low sexy voice breathed against the back of her neck.

Her muscles bunched and then relaxed when she realized who was behind her. With a sigh, she leaned back against a solid chest, inhaling the scent of musky cologne and male.

Roger. The man of her dreams. The man destined to stay in her dreams. Other than the stolen kisses in the emergency room hallway that managed to graduate into some particularly heavy groping sessions in this supply closet, she'd done little else but fantasize about this man. How she'd love to do a lot more, maybe spend an entire night together—naked.

His breath stirred the hairs that had fallen loose from the neat ponytail she'd started the night with. Arms circled around her middle, rising beneath her breasts.

"Pervert," she whispered and pressed her bottom against the hard ridge behind his uniform trousers. While his hands slipped beneath her scrub shirt and lacy bra, she reached behind her to cup his ass. God, how she wanted him. "You're going to get me fired."

"Then we'll have time to do more of this." His tongue curled around her earlobe and he sucked it into his mouth, nibbling gently with his teeth.

"Um, perhaps I could live on sex alone?" She turned in his arms. "Who needs food or a roof over my head, when I can have all this?"

"Now you're thinking."

"Yeah, but it's time to quit thinking and start…" she pressed her lips to his, cutting off further conversation. Her time was short. She'd better make good use of it.

He pushed her bra up over her breasts and tweaked her nipples between his thumb and forefingers. Pressing his cheek against her hair, he inhaled. "You smell like heaven."

She laughed. "How can you smell anything over the disinfectant and dirty mops?"

"I can, when I'm this close." He nudged a knee between her legs, rubbing his thigh against her cunt.

When his leg touched her there, all the air whooshed out of her lungs and she clung to him.

A hand rose to cup her face in the darkness, his lips descending to claim hers in a long scorching kiss. While his tongue toyed and dueled with hers, blunt-tipped fingers slid once more beneath her shirt.

She tugged the buttons open on his uniform to comb her fingers through his chest hairs, except a cotton t-shirt stood in the way. Julie plucked at it.

"You have too many clothes on." Short of pulling his shirt and t-shirt from his waistband she had to content herself with sliding her fingers between his uniform and the t-shirt. When she found the hard little knots of his nipples beneath the soft cotton, she tweaked.

The hard ridge of his cock rocked against her belly. "Your clothes are much more accessible to play." He pushed his hands beneath the elastic waistband of her scrubs and burrowed into the silky bikini underwear to the furry mound at the juncture of her thighs.

"I CAN'T BELIEVE we're doing this in a janitor's closet." Despite her words, her legs spread to give him more maneuvering room.

"I'd rather have you in my bed." With his index finger, he parted the thick folds and stroked the cleft between.

Julie moaned, her back arching, pressing her into his hand. "What if someone comes?" she gasped.

"What if you come?" He paused, his fingers cupping her sex lightly. "Do you want me to stop?"

"Are you kidding?" She grabbed his arm and pushed him deeper. "If you stop now, I'll die."

He needed no further encouragement. Like a mechanic, he dipped his finger in to test how slick and lubricated she was. "God, you're wet." He dragged creamy juices up to that sensitive nub and flicked it until Julie leaned into him, gasping. Raw need filled her, nerves jumping with every stroke, until she was spiraling up and over the edge, her pelvis jerking her release. Then she pressed her forehead to his chest. "Oh, God." With a long deep breath, she blew out in a sharp stream against his neck. "Now, your turn."

She was fumbling with his belt buckle when the door handle jerked.

"What the hell?" A male voice muttered on the other side.

Julie froze for a moment. Then her fingers dropped from his zipper. "Shit. My boss will fire me on the spot if she catches me in here with you."

"Don't sweat it, sounded more like a man than a woman out there."

"Yeah, but he might go to her for the key to the closet." She spun around in the dark, straightening her clothes, tugging her bra down over her breasts.

Roger buckled his belt and was buttoning his shirt when the door swung open.

"Kim!" Julie fell out of the closet and hugged her friend. "Thank God it's you."

"Don't thank me now, the battle-axe is on the warpath, and she's looking for you. Run the other way while I get Mr. Hot-and-Bothered out the back."

"Thanks, Kim." She turned back to Roger and sighed. "At the risk of sounding trite, we have got to stop meeting this way."

"I know." He pressed a kiss to her forehead. "Actually, that's why I came by."

Julie's gaze darted up and down the hallway before returning to him. "Oh yeah?"

"I have tomorrow night off."

"You do?" She squealed and clapped a hand over her mouth. "So do I!"

"I know." A slow, sexy grin slid across his face and he waggled his eyebrows.

"And?" Was he going to ask her out on a real date? Julie sent a silent prayer heavenward. Please, please, please…

He shrugged and started to turn away, a wicked gleam in his eyes. "I just thought I'd let you know."

Julie punched his arm. "What do I have to do? Beg?"

"For what?"

"You're impossible."

"Yeah, I am, aren't I?" He grinned.

Kim glanced around. "You two better figure it out quick, here she comes."

"How about it?" He grabbed her and pressed the hard ridge of his cock against her belly. "Tomorrow? A real date? I have reservations at the Red Lantern."

"Yes!" She flung her arms around his neck and kissed him full on the mouth and let him go just as quickly. "A real date, with food, and candles and se—" Kim nudged her in the back hard enough she stumbled into Roger.

"Nurse Lindeman," Kim said behind her. "Julie

was just questioning Mr. Decker about the psych case he brought in."

Roger's lips twitched as if he forced back the smile threatening to take over his face.

The heat in Julie's cheeks deepened and she struggled with words. "Uh…yes…I was just questioning Mr. Decker about the…uh—"

"Psych case in Room 2. But now she's done, right, Julie? Mr. Marley is waiting in Room 2. Mustn't keep him waiting, must we. No ma'am." Kim hustled Julie past the head nurse and continued toward the room with the psych case.

Nurse Lindeman let them go, but as Julie passed her, she noted how her eyes narrowed and she nailed Roger with a piercing glare. "Aren't you the same cop that's been hanging around lately?"

"Come on." Kim tugged Julie down the hallway.

"But she'll chew him up and spit him out." Julie didn't feel right leaving Roger to handle Nurse Lindeman by himself.

"He's a big boy, he can manage all by himself. Besides, you have to fill me in on all the juicy details.

Julie's cheeks warmed as she recalled just how juicy the details had been. "No way."

"Hey, how am I supposed to live vicariously through you if you don't share?" Kim shoved her through the doorway.

"Get your own life!" With a last glance at Roger, Julie caught him winking at her over Nurse Lindeman's head. Tomorrow night was going to be great.

She was finally going to have a real date, with real sex, and the best part was that she'd be with Roger.

"What's this about a psych case?" Nurse Lindeman was asking.

After Julie disappeared through a doorway, Roger dragged his gaze back to the woman in front of him.

"Ma'am?" What had she asked? He couldn't recall. Not after watching Julie's ass twitch all the way down the hall. So, he smiled his most charming smile, the one he reserved for the politicians' wives.

"If you'd get your mind off my nurse's ass for a moment, we could both do our jobs."

Her sharp words brought him back in focus. "Bob Marley, the guy I brought in a few minutes ago, was caught trying to stab some poor bum with a wooden stake."

"Huh? Why the hell did you bring him here? You should have taken him down to the station and booked him on assault charges."

Roger ignored the head nurse's attempt to tell him how to do his job. "I would have, except he sounded hysterical, a little deranged. I thought maybe you guys could test him for drugs or something. He was pretty upset, to the point of crazy. We had to strap him down. I left him with the doctor."

"Great. Just what we need. A nutcase stirring up trouble in my emergency room. Anything else you'd like to tell me?" Nurse Lindeman crossed her arms over her chest and her brows rose high on her forehead.

He knew what she wanted, but he avoided any mention of Julie. Although he'd like more time with her, he didn't want to get her fired from her job. "Yeah, Mr. Marley was screaming something about being a slayer and his job was to rid the world of vampires." Roger shrugged and grinned. "He's a live one."

"Thanks." Nurse Lindeman's lips twisted. "Remind me to return the favor some time."

"Don't mention it," he said lightly and turned to leave, but a hand caught his arm.

"By the way," she touched a finger to his chest. "Your buttons are mismatched and your fly is open." She turned away, a smile stretching across her face, a sparkle lighting her eyes.

Roger glanced down.

Busted.

For a moment he wished he could be swallowed by the floor, his face burned all the way out to the tips of his ears. Now he knew what was more embarrassing than getting caught in the act. Getting caught with your fly down by the head nurse.

Oh well, shit happens. He just hoped he didn't get Julie in too much trouble. Roger quickly adjusted the offending buttons and zipper. He couldn't get too bent, he had a date with Julie tomorrow night. A real, honest-to-God date. Not just a quick feel in the janitor's closet.

He rubbed his hands together and headed for his squad car and his waiting partner.

Chase leaned against the driver's door talking with a pretty little blonde in white scrubs and a blue lab coat. When he saw Roger, he straightened. "About time you showed up, partner." He gathered the blonde in his arms and kissed her like he was going to crawl down her throat or throw her on the hood of the squad car and bang her there. "I'll see you later, baby."

When he let her go, she staggered backward, her eyes glazed and a hand fluttering to her lips. "Call me?"

He winked. "You bet."

As he climbed into the passenger side of the squad car, Roger's lips twisted.

Chase eased behind the wheel and started the engine.

"You aren't going to call her, are you?" Roger's words were more of a statement than a question.

"Nope."

"Why do you do that?" He could imagine Julie's reaction if he kissed her like that and didn't call later. She'd be hurt, disappointed and then angry.

"Do what?"

"Kiss and run."

"You're one to be talking." Chase shot him a look, complete with raised eyebrows. "How long has your divorce been final?"

"Two years."

"And you've been out on how many dates?"

"None," he said. "But that's different. I haven't wanted to go out with another woman, until now."

"Buddy, you either qualify as a saint or deserve the dumbass-of-the-year award. I couldn't go two weeks without sex, much less two years." Chase slammed the car in drive and pulled out of the parking area into traffic.

Roger stared at the blur of streetlights skimming past his window. Two years. Two years since his marriage fell apart. Two years since he'd caught his wife sleeping with another cop. He hadn't trusted any woman since.

Until Julie. His fingers still tingled from the warmth and silkiness of her skin. He couldn't wait until tomorrow night. After a candlelit dinner at her favorite restaurant, they'd go back to his apartment for a little dessert. Sensuous music and soft lighting ought to set the mood for his planned seduction. He wanted to bury himself in Julie and forget how much his ex-wife's deception had hurt.

Julie, the angel in nurse's clothing. Kind, gentle Julie with her strawberry blonde hair and pale, soft skin was just what he needed to get over Susan. His Julie would never lie to him like Susan had. She'd never lie to him or see another man on the side.

"So what did you decide? Are you a saint or a dumbass?" Chase's voice brought him back to the interior of the squad car.

"Neither."

"So when are you going to get into that nurse's pants? What's her name? Julia?"

"It's Julie and tomorrow. I mean, I asked her out tomorrow. But that doesn't mean I'm going to get into her pants." Although that's exactly where he'd been only moments before, in his mind.

"Then you're definitely a dumbass."

The radios on their shoulders squawked. "All units in the vicinity of Main and Lamar Streets, assault in progress. Please respond."

"That's us." Roger pressed the talk button on his radio to inform the dispatcher they'd take the call and their estimated time of arrival. Then he settled back in his seat, glad the diversion had taken Chase's mind off the subject of Julie and her pants.

When the squad car stopped in the location given, Roger didn't see anyone at first. "Do you think it was a crank call?"

"I think I saw movement in that alley. Let's go." Chase shoved the car in park and leapt out, drawing the Glock from his holster.

Before Chase could round the car, Roger took off at a dead run toward the alley, hugging the buildings along the sidewalk. Adrenaline packed his veins, shooting blood to his brain, clearing his hearing, vision and thinking processes to hone in on his quarry. This was the reason he loved his job. Not the nights of boring patrols, hauling in drunks or cleaning up prostitutes.

No, he loved going after the bad guys and

bringing them down. Face it. He was a thrill junkie. The night shift was the best place to find them.

When he reached the alley, he stood with his back to the wall and waited for Chase to catch up. With a nod toward his partner, he stepped into the dark passage. A shadow moved beside a dumpster. It appeared to be a man. A man carrying another person. A woman.

"Halt! Or I'll shoot!"

A wicked rumble erupted from the shadows and built into the sound of laughter, a deep masculine laugh. The shadow straightened, the laughter stopped and piercing red eyes turned toward Roger. "Toy cops."

"Let her go." Roger called out.

"By all means." The stranger dropped the body he was holding. It fell to the pavement with a dull *whomp*. "Now what? Gonna arrest me?"

"Step to the side and lay face to the ground."

"No, I don't think so. I don't like to play by the rules."

Before Roger could react, the man leapt the six yards between them in one bound.

His finger squeezed on the trigger and his Glock erupted into the man's belly.

The man only laughed, seized Roger's weapon and slung it to the side.

Chase unloaded six rounds in rapid succession into the man's chest.

Other than jerking at the impact, the bullets did nothing but make holes through his body.

He lifted Roger by the front of his uniform and slung him ten feet across the pavement. He landed in the street on his back, all the wind knocked from his lungs, his head pounding hard against the asphalt.

Chase landed beside him.

The stranger stared down at them, his white-blond hair standing up straight in ragged spikes. A smile crept across his face. "I just stopped for a snack. Thanks for the entertainment." Then the man was gone so fast Roger had to blink to make sure his vision wasn't impaired by the fall.

Recovering first, Roger sucked air into his lungs in a desperate gasp. "Fuck! What was that?"

When Chase didn't answer right away, Roger rolled over to check him out. "You all right, buddy?"

His partner pressed a hand to his head. "Did you get the number of that truck that hit me?"

"No shit. I unloaded on him and the bullets didn't even faze him." Roger stared into the darkness.

"That was one scary son of a bitch."

"Yeah. I'm beginning to rethink my career choice."

THANK GOD FOR 3:00 A.M. Julie slipped into her sweater, grabbed her purse and headed for the exit. On her way out, she passed by her dark-haired friend leading a patient into an exam room. "See ya the day after tomorrow, Kim."

"Don't do anything I wouldn't do on your really hot date the Cop Candy."

Julie paused, and rested her hands on her hips. "Is there anything you wouldn't do?"

With a frown and a glance at the ceiling, Kim answered, "Nope. Nothing I can think of. So that leaves it wide open. Use your imagination."

Julie turned to leave, a smile on her face.

"Hey," Kim called after her.

"More advice?" Julie fisted a hand on one hip.

"If you need to borrow my Kama Sutra book, just stop by tomorrow anytime."

The old lady leaning on Kim nodded. "That Kama Sutra book saved my marriage, it did. Although some of those positions are physically impossible at my age."

Julie ducked out the side door to the sound of Kim's giggles.

Out in the parking garage, Julie climbed into her car and turned the key.

Click.

She tried again.

Click.

She checked the battery gauge. "Ah, shit."

Her battery was deader than dead.

"Fuck!"

Although she only lived four blocks from the hospital, the thought of walking home on her aching feet brought tears to her eyes. The hospital parking lot was completely empty of people. She could wait another two hours until Kim got off, or call a cab. Hell, she could walk her butt home faster than it would take a cab to get there.

As she climbed out of her car, and slung her purse over her shoulder, every bone and muscle in her body sagged.

Damn cars. Why couldn't they break down at a more opportune time, like on the way to work when her feet didn't hurt?

She strode down the garage ramp and out onto the sidewalk, working up anger as she walked. No, mechanical problems had to wait until frickin' three o'clock in the morning when not a single car passed by. When only the drunks and bums wandered around. She sure as hell hoped they wouldn't bother her on her way home. Thank goodness there was no such thing as the monsters that Bob Marley had ranted about earlier. She owed Roger for that one. The man was delusional. All his talk about vampires and demons.

Good thing Julie didn't believe in all that nonsense.

Because if she did, she'd be a little afraid tonight. She glanced up at the full moon ringed in an eerie red glow. Yup. A more superstitious woman would be running back to the hospital and waiting for Kim to get off to bum a ride home. But not Julie. She was the levelheaded one. Not easily spooked.

"No, sir. I don't believe in all that Goth vampire shit."

Just as she spoke the words out loud, a man appeared in front of her. A very tall, broad-shouldered man with blond, spiked hair and dark eyes. No. Make that red eyes. He reminded her of a bulkier Spike from a Buffy rerun.

"Maybe you should believe," he said, his voice more a growl than anything else.

Julie dropped back a step, swallowed a scream and said the first thing that came to her mind. "Geesh! You shouldn't jump out at people in the middle of the night. I could have died of a heart attack."

"I doubt you'll die of a heart attack tonight."

"Only because I'm in pretty good shape and eat healthy." She stared hard at him, though her pulse beat at an erratic rate. This man, with all his bulging muscles, could

easily take her, rape her or anything else he had a mind to. She was a lone woman armed only with her purse.

Her hand shifted to the bag. She did have a small canister of mace at the bottom of her oversized bag, if she could get to it before he killed her.

"If you want money, you can have whatever is in my wallet. I'll get it." Like he couldn't see right through her ruse? She jammed her hand inside her handbag and rummaged frantically.

He plucked the purse from her shoulder and tossed it and the mace several yards away.

"Okaaayyy. I guess I'll just have to use my black belt in karate." She dropped into a crouch, her hands in chop position and yelled like she'd seen the bad guys do in the Jackie Chan flicks. Not that she knew any more than that. But maybe she could bluff her way out of a potentially lose-lose situation.

Where the hell was a cop when you needed one? Where was Roger? He should still be on duty. Why couldn't he drive by about now and rescue her? "So? What's it gonna be? Are you going to let me by without a hassle, or am I going to have to take you down?" *Please let me by. Please.*

CHAPTER 2

"Julie? Julie, wake up!"

What? She was in such a dead sleep, she could barely push her eyelids open. When she did, she stared up at a familiar face. "William? What are you doing in my apartment?" Julie pushed against her bed, only she didn't feel the soft, clean Laura Ashley sheets. Instead, she felt the grit of pavement and grime beneath her hands. "What the hell?"

As her vision cleared, she focused on William Fagan, the guy who lived in the apartment across the hallway from her in the old colonial house on Sixth Street. The gray light of predawn filtered through the buildings to barely illuminate the alley in which she lay flat on her face on the dirty pavement. "Where am I?"

"You're about three blocks from home and we need to get there in a hurry."

"What happened?" She sat up, brushing gravel from her cheek.

"I'll explain what I know when we get you inside. But if we don't get you home soon, you'll fry." He scooped an arm beneath her shoulders and hefted her to an upright position. "Come on."

Julie sprang to her feet, feeling strangely light and bouncy for having slept on the pavement. What the hell was going on? Before she could ask another question, William took off at a run, her hand still in his.

Because she hadn't made a move to follow, he practically jerked her arm out of socket. Once she got her running legs going, she had no trouble keeping his pace, which was strange in itself. She hadn't jogged or worked out on a regular basis in months. The night shift had thrown her workout schedule completely off. By all rights, she should be gasping for air. But she wasn't. In fact, she was barely breathing hard at all. "What's the rush?"

"No time to explain," he called over his shoulder. "Hurry!"

The sky changed from dull, battleship gray to the vibrant pinks, purples and orange of dawn just as they arrived in front of the huge old house that had been divided into six apartments. As the sun popped over the horizon and cast its first rays of light onto her and William, she could feel a terrible burning sensation ripping across her exposed skin. Tingling, turned to prickling and finally to searing and she smelled the distinct odor of burning flesh. *Her burning flesh.*

William yanked the front door open and shoved her inside. He pushed her so hard, she sprawled on the floor, sliding several feet before she stopped. "Hey, you don't have to be so rough!"

He slammed the door closed behind him and collapsed against the heavy wood paneling. "Whew! That was close."

"Close to what?" Julie pushed to her feet and dusted the grit from her hands. "I thought you were such a nice neighbor. What's with slamming me to the ground? That's no way to treat a lady."

"Honey, I hate to break it to you. But you're no lady."

"That's not funny." When William only stared at her, Julie's back straightened, anger rising in the form of a blood rush to her head. "I beg your pardon."

"Beg all you want, but as of early this morning, you're no longer a lady." He hooked her elbow and ushered her to the staircase leading to the second level of the house and their apartments. "If you'll step into my apartment, I'll fill you in."

She planted her feet against the smooth black and white tiles of the foyer, bringing William to a halt. Then she shook his hand free of her elbow. "I'm not going anywhere with someone who tells me I'm no longer a lady. I'll have you know, I don't sleep around. In fact, I haven't had sex in…well…that's none of your business." *Three years, three loooonnnng years*. But that was about to change. Tonight. She had a date.

"I'm not talking about sex." He reached for her arm again.

Julie pulled away. "If you're not talking about sex, then what *are* you talking about? Unless you know about a sex change operation I might have had in the few short hours I was unconscious, I'm still a woman and therefore—"

"Could you shut up long enough to get up the stairs?" William left her standing in the hallway and took the steps two at a time. "Sheesh, woman."

"Ah hah! You admit it. I am a woman, therefore a lady." She followed behind him. Taking the same steps he did, two at a time. She never took steps two at a time. Normally, she was wheezing and gasping for air as she climbed steps one at a time, never mind two at a time. But here she was taking two and…she tried it…three steps at a time. No problem. Maybe she should get conked on the head more often. It beat the hell out of a regular workout routine.

Much as she'd like to get a shower and head for bed, she needed to know a few things. "By the way, William, why was I sleeping in an alley like a homeless person?"

He waited for her to cross his threshold, and then he closed his door and pushed the bolt home. "Now that we're inside and don't stand the chance of being seen or overheard, I can fill you in. Why you couldn't just keep quiet until we got here, I don't know." He took a deep breath and stared down at her.

"I never was very good at surprises and I get the feeling you're about to surprise me. I'm not going to like the surprise, am I?"

With a worried frown, William blew out a long, steady breath. "Maybe you better sit down."

Uh-oh. She didn't like the way he was stalling. "What, did the landlord evict me and I stumbled out into the street, devastated and homeless?"

"No, nothing as simple as that."

"That's simple?" Double uh-oh. She perched on the edge of his bomber-jacket brown leather sofa. "Okay, I'm sitting. Just tell me already. I'm dying here."

"You can't die, Julie. You're already dead."

Her mouth dropped open. "Huh?" Who was he trying to kid? She was a walking, talking, gawking person sitting in his living room. "Uh, William. Have you been smoking some wacky weed or something? Hellooooo. If I'm here talking to you, how can I be dead?"

"It's complicated."

"Try me."

"Then keep an open mind." His eyebrows dropped toward the bridge of his nose in a V.

"I'm open."

"Julie, last night, you were turned."

"Turned?" She grasped for any possible meaning

she could come up with for the unfamiliar phrase. "Like a fruit held too long on the branch turned?"

"No."

"Like coming out of the closet gay turned?"

"No."

"I give up." She sat back against the couch, her arms crossing over her chest. "What do you mean?"

"Turned as in from human to vampire."

She could have caught flies as low as her jaw dropped. "William, I've known you, what, a year and a half, maybe?"

"Yeah."

"And this is the first time you've ever done anything remotely weird."

"So?"

"So." She pushed up from the couch and strode for the door. "I'll cut you a break. I'm going home to shower and bed. When I wake up, maybe we can start this conversation all over. 'Cause I know you didn't just say I've been turned to a vampire,

and I know you're not crazy. I'm counting it as a really bizarre nightmare I'll wake up from after a decent amount of sleep."

William appeared in front of her, blocking her path to the doorway. "It's true."

Wait a minute. One minute he was behind her at the couch. Now he was in front of her. When had he made the trip? Had she blinked? She shook her head.

He grinned. "It's one of the perks."

"What's one of the perks? And perks of what?"

"Speed. Vampires are really fast."

She put a hand up. "No, wait, forget I asked. I don't want to hear any more trash talk about vampires. You know and I know they don't exist. You sound like that Bob Marley guy we sedated at the hospital earlier. He was ranting about vampires loose on the streets of Houston."

"They are."

"But everyone knows vampires are just a bizarre manifestation of some writers' fancy. Like were-wolves and demons."

"They exist too." William's face set in grim lines.

Julie shook her head, having a hard time grasping reality. "You do that so well."

"What?"

"The straight-faced thing." Julie laughed out loud and looked around the room. "All right Kim, you can come out now. I know you're hiding back there somewhere."

The confused expression on William's face looked very real. "Kim who?"

"My practical joking friend from the hospital. That's who." Julie poked a finger into William's chest. "She put you up to this, didn't she?"

Her neighbor grabbed her finger and pulled her hand into his. "Look, Julie. This is a lot to take in all at once. But no kidding. You're a vampire. And as a vampire, there are certain, shall I say, rules you have to follow. The immortality thing is only if you follow the rules."

Julie's heart sank into her belly as dread washed over her like a mudslide in California. "You're not joking are you?"

"I'm sorry to say, no."

"But how?" She sank onto the couch staring up at him as his words sank deeper.

"Come with me." He grabbed her hand and marched her into his bathroom. When Julie stood in front of the mirror, William lifted the hair away from her neck.

"See the bite marks on your neck?"

"Shit." She leaned closer, rubbing at the six puncture wounds scattered across the column of her throat in sets of two, conveniently aligned with her jugular vein. "Where the hell did these come from?"

"A vampire must have gotten you last night."

"If I am a vampire, how come I can see myself in the mirror and where are my fangs?"

With a chuckle, William shook his head. "The mirror thing is a myth. The fangs will fill in by tomorrow night."

She turned her head to stare at the sets of puncture wounds. "You sure these aren't spider bites?" she asked weakly.

His apologetic smile had more of an impact than any words he could have spoken.

That sick feeling in her gut intensified as an image of the dark man with the spiky blond hair blocking her path last night wedged its way into her fuzzy memories. "Does this have something to do with that man I ran into on my way home?"

"Probably. I received word another human got nailed, so I came out looking and found you." With a nod toward the mirror, William noted, "You see the blood on your lips?"

Her hand rose to touch the dried blood. "What's this?"

"That would be the vampire's blood. He made you drink his blood in order to turn you."

As if burned by a hot iron, she jerked her finger away from the blood and bent over the sink, scrubbing at the spot with clean, cool water. She reached for a towel.

William turned her toward him, towel in hand, and patted her face dry. "Do you remember what he looked like?"

Julie squeezed her eyes shut and thought hard. "White-blond hair, very tall and I remember this…he had red eyes." She opened her eyes and stared at William. "You think he did this to me?" Was she really a vampire?

"Sounds like one of the rogue vampires we've been looking for."

"One?" Julie shook her head. "You mean there are more?"

"Yes, there are hundreds of vampires in Houston. Ever since Hurricane Katrina, they've spread from New Orleans to other major cities across the U.S."

No, this couldn't be true. "I'm not believing this. Vampires don't exist in real life."

"No, but they exist in death."

"And I'm a vampire? A real live vampire?"

"Ahem," William cleared his throat. "Not live. Not really. You're considered one of the living dead."

"But what about my life? My job. My family?" She stared up at him as she realized how all the threads of her former existence were unraveling around her.

"It's totally up to you what you do about your family and your job. You may choose to disappear and start over somewhere else or continue on as though nothing's different." He held up a finger. "With some exceptions."

"Exceptions." The world was crashing around her ears and William was talking about exceptions. She had trouble even focusing on what he was saying.

"You can't go out in daylight or you'll fry into a crispy critter and die."

"No more sunrises, or sunbathing in the nude." Not like she'd get up early enough to watch a sunrise. But she'd always dreamed of sunbathing on some Greek island

absolutely naked. Then again, when would she make enough money to go to the Greek Islands?

William droned on. "Avoid falling on or being pierced with sharp wooden objects, silver knives or bullets. Any of these items through the heart are deadly to a vampire."

"What if I stab myself with a pencil?" she asked, not sure it was really her voice.

"As long as it's not through the heart, you're okay. But if it makes you feel better, use pens or mechanical pencils. It's best to feed at least every other day to keep up your strength."

"Feed? As in sucking blood from other people?" Her stomach churned. "Ewwww."

"Yes. But the upside is you'll have superhuman strength. You'll be stronger than Arnold Schwarzenegger and Vin Diesel put together."

"Really?" Perhaps there was an upside to this vampire thing. She could quit worrying about putting her back out when helping patients in the hospital. "My job! What about my job?"

"I suggest you put in for permanent night shift to avoid daylight hours."

"I can keep my job? They won't fire me or anything?"

"Not unless you tell them you're a vampire. In which case, they'll commit you to the psych ward or give you over to science to dissect."

"Immortality spent in a padded room?" Julie laughed, her world was spinning around her completely out of control and she was making jokes. Hell, the joke was on her!

"Exactly. We in the vampire community keep knowledge of our identity to ourselves and a limited few we can trust."

Huh? "So, you're a vampire?" And all this time she'd never even suspected. "How?"

"I was turned over a century ago by a lovely lady in Boston." He sighed. "She truly was a beauty. Dark hair and brown eyes that could melt you on the spot."

"What happened to her?"

"Someone ratted on her and they staked her." A flash of something, pain maybe, crossed his eyes before he turned his attention back to her. "You'll be okay. And I'm just across the hall if you need anything."

"Like?"

"You might need some help with your first feeding."

"Do I really have to bite someone? I can't imagine walking up to a stranger and saying, 'Excuse me, could you spare some blood?'"

William laughed. "It's not quite done that way."

"Then how?" She really was clueless, and if she wanted to survive, she'd have to learn. Wow. Was she really buying into all this? Julie Taylor? A vampire? Never to see the light of day again? "Who did this to me?"

"By your description, I'd bet it was a two-hundred-year-old vampire named Luke Hester. He's been a bit out of control over the past couple weeks. Gives the rest of us a bad name."

"Luke Hester?" A shudder snaked its way down her spine as the memory of that big man in the alley surfaced from the fog of the previous night. "But he had red eyes? Why don't you?" She spun toward the mirror and breathed a sigh of relief when the reflection still showed green eyes. "Or me for that matter?"

"The red eyes come from turning bad. He came over from England before I was turned and basically has been causing trouble since. But lately more so than usual."

"So Bob Marley wasn't crazy."

"Bob Marley?"

"He said he was a vampire hunter. When they brought him in, he was talking nonsense about vampires on the rampage and how he was determined to kill every last one of them. We thought he was on drugs, but he tested clean. So we committed him for psychological evaluation. Poor guy was right."

"Good thing you have him locked up. He could be dangerous to the good vampires as well as the bad ones."

"You mean there are good ones?" she asked.

"Eh-hem. Excuse me. There is yours truly." William spread his arms wide. "The majority of the vampires live among the humans. It's vamps like Luke who make problems for us all."

"Should I be worried about this rogue vampire? I mean, he's already done the damage." She turned her head to the side and stared at the wounds.

"Only if he comes back for you. Sometimes, when a vampire turns you, he can claim you as his mate. That hasn't happened in a long time. But I'd stay away from Luke if I were you."

"No problem." If memory served her correctly, he was a pretty scary kinda guy. "Won't my superhuman strength help me out where he's concerned?"

"Some. But he's been at it longer. He'll be twice as strong as you."

Julie snapped her fingers. "Damn."

William pushed a hand through his wavy blond hair. "I'm beat and it's about time for some sleep. If you need anything, don't hesitate to ask."

"Thanks. I don't know what I'd have done without your help out there."

"You'd have fried."

"Yeah." She stood and strode for the door. "I guess I'll get cleaned up and get some sleep. That's what vampires do during the day, huh?"

"Pretty much. Although some get around in their day jobs with a lot of prior planning and S.A.T.s"

Julie's mind whirled with the new terminology and rules. "S.A.T.s? What are those?"

"Sun avoidance techniques."

For the first time since she'd known William, she noted the closed blinds and drawn drapes over the windows. Why hadn't she noticed before? "They really can get around during the day and hold a job?"

"Yeah, but I don't recommend it for the neophytes."

"Okay." She hated to step out the door. All this was new to her and William was her only ally in a world gone bizarre. "Thanks again." With nothing left to say or any reason to stall, she stepped across the hallway and into her apartment.

Sunlight streamed through her windows and she squinted, her eyes burning. First things first, she'd have to close all the blinds. After accomplishing that task with minimal scorching, she headed for the bathroom and stood in front of the mirror examining her neck. The puncture wounds were already healing, but still visible.

Damn. She was a vampire. Tears welled in her eyes and slipped down her cheeks. Damn.

How was she going to tell her folks? Her boss? Kim?

The phone rang.

What should she do? Should she answer like nothing out of the ordinary? She could say, "Hello, this is Julie. I'm dead. How are you?"

On the third ring, she grabbed the receiver with no idea what she was going to say to whoever was on the line.

"Hey, beautiful."

Oh geez! "Roger?"

"You sound surprised. Did I wake you?"

"No!" What should she do? What should she say?

"I just got off work and remembered we didn't set a time."

"Time?" What was wrong with her? Did becoming a vampire take away her brain capacity?

"For our date?" Roger chuckled. "You didn't change your mind did you?"

Change her mind? She wanted to shout, "Hell no!" But, given the circumstances, shouldn't she cancel? "Hell no!" she said before she could think beyond those two words.

"Good. For a moment there, I thought I'd lost you."

For all intents and purposes he had. She was a dead woman. He was a living, breathing, vegetable-and-ice-cream-eating human. What the hell did they have in common after the events of this morning? Nothing! "No, you didn't lose me."

"I'm glad. Because I have plans for a special dinner followed by dessert at my place."

Dinner? Oh God! Hey, could she say that? Wasn't she one of the damned? Would God ever forgive her? Was she going to hell when she died? Oh wait, she was already dead. Would she go to hell when she got dusted?

Thoughts tumbled in Julie's head, refusing to take root, become coherent. With a decided yank, she pulled her mind back to dinner. What the hell could she eat? She scribbled on a pad by the phone, "Ask William what vampires can eat besides blood and am I going to hell?" Both questions made her shiver.

"So I'll pick you up at six?"

"Sounds great." No wait. What was that one rule? "Will the sun be down by then?"

"I don't think so. Why?"

"Uh, no reason." Six was not an option. "Could you pick me up at seven? I'm thinking I could use an extra hour of beauty sleep." The sun should be down by then. The days wouldn't get longer until closer to June.

"Not that you need the extra hour. You're beautiful just as you are. But I'd be happy to pick you up at seven."

"Oh and Roger?" Should she tell him before the date? That way he had a choice as to whether or not to go out with a dead woman.

"Yes, gorgeous?"

Her toes curled at the endearment. Maybe telling him now wasn't such a good idea. A subject like "I'm a bloodsucking vampire" might be better broached in person over a glass of wine. "I can't wait to see you." Make that an entire bottle of wine.

"Me too. Finally." He laughed again. "I thought we'd never actually have a real date."

"Me either," she said, a flicker of guilt growing into a major head-banger. They still wouldn't be having a real date. But Roger didn't have to know that. Not yet, anyway. She'd waited too long for this date, she'd be damned if she missed it. No wait…she was damned. Again, Roger didn't have to know that. Not yet.

"And, baby, we're not going to let anything get in our way of a good time."

"Right. See ya tonight." Oh boy, was she in for an interesting evening. Last night, she'd only been thinking about how she could seduce Roger within the first five minutes of their date. Now, she wanted him more than ever, but her thoughts would be tied up with how to be a vampire and not blow it! She needed to talk to William before she went out.

But first, sleep. Apparently, being immortal didn't mean you could go without sleep. It just meant always sleeping during the day. No change there. Especially having worked the night shift for the past three months. Just because she was a vampire didn't mean her life had to change, did it?

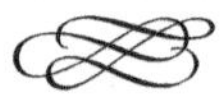

CHAPTER 3

After the third ring, Julie's answering machine picked up, "Hi, this is Julie. Leave a message." A beep and then—

"Answer the phone for Heaven's sakes!" Kim's voice erupted with a mechanical twang.

Julie buried her head beneath the pillow and moaned. "What's Heaven got to do with it, anyway?"

"I know you're home, so don't ignore me. It's six-thirty and you haven't answered your phone all day. Did you and Cop Candy find each other last night? Want me to go away? Okay, I've made enough inane conversation. You're probably in the shower anyway. Call me."

Before Kim could hang up, Julie's hand shot out from beneath the covers and snatched the phone. Where had that little burst of energy come from? Oh yeah, vampires are speedy. "I'm here."

"Julie?"

"I think so."

"What's wrong? You don't sound like yourself." Kim smacked her gum into the receiver. "You sound like death warmed over."

"You got that right."

"Don't tell me you're sick and can't make your date?" With a snort, Kim said, "I thought nothing short of death would keep you and Badge Boy away from the sheets tonight."

If only she knew. "No, I'm fine, just slept in. What time did you say it was?"

"Six-thirty, Sleeping Beauty."

"Six-thirty!" Julie flung the pillow, blankets and half the items on her nightstand halfway across the room as she leapt from bed. "Crap! He'll be here in less than thirty minutes and I haven't even had a shower!"

"You can thank me later," Kim's smug voice sounded over the line.

"How should I fix my hair? What'll I wear? Hell, what'll I eat?" Julie's voice rose as she listed the questions jumbled in her mind. Number one being how could she pull off the biggest lie ever. "I have to go."

"Relax, girlfriend! You'll do fine."

Julie could picture Kim rolling her eyeliner-ringed eyes. "Easy for you to say." *You're not the dead woman.*

"By the way, before you hang up on me, I thought you'd like to know. That psych case your boyfriend brought in last night walked out of here sometime after you left."

Kim's words penetrated Julie's panic and made her grip the phone until she was sure the plastic would crack. "He did? How? I thought we had him pretty well sedated."

"Apparently not. He wasn't nearly as sedated or secured as we thought. He slipped through the restraints and waltzed out of here when no one was looking."

Great. Just what she needed. Along about the time she was trying to get used to the idea she was a vampire, the vampire-slayer-psycho-dude was on the loose in the city. *What else could possibly go wrong?*

Her doorbell rang.

I had to ask.

All the way to her front door Julie muttered beneath her breath, "Please don't let it be Roger thirty minutes early…pulleeeze!"

When she'd crossed the living area and pressed her eye to the peephole, she let go of the breath she'd been holding. William bent and looked back at her through the tiny opening.

"Julie? Is that you?" The door shook.

Before he could shake the door again Julie flung it aside, grabbed his arm and jerked him inside slamming the door behind him.

"Nice to see you too." A smile quirked the corners of William's mouth.

"I have thirty—" Julie glanced at the clock on the

wall and gasped. "Make that twenty minutes before my date arrives." She grabbed his arm in a death grip. "What do I do? How do I get around? What do I eat? Are there any other side effects to being a vamp?"

"Whoa! Hold on a minute." William held his hands up to ward off her barrage of questions. "One question at a time."

"One question at a time? Don't you understand? I have a date with a man!" No, that didn't sound good. Desperate, more like. Julie sucked in a deep breath and rolled her shoulders. There. Now that she had a grip...she grabbed William's arms and shook him. "What do I do?"

William's rich laughter filled her apartment. "It's okay, Julie. All you have to do is act natural. Other than being a vampire, you're still you."

"Other than—are you freakin' out of your mind?" She threw herself away from him and stomped across the room and back. "I'm a stinkin' vampire!"

A frown settled between William's brows. "I resemble that." Before she could turn and walk away for her second pass at pacing, he placed both hands on her shoulders and stared into her eyes. "Julie, most of us didn't *ask* to be vampires, but you can't undo what was done. You have to learn to deal with it."

The intensity of his blue eyes poked through the bubble of extreme anxiety pressing in around Julie and she nodded. "Okay. But you have to help me."

"I'll do all I can." He let go of her shoulders and clapped his hands together. "Shoot."

"First question, what should I do about my date? And speaking of date, I have to get a shower!" Julie dashed for her bathroom, grabbing fresh black lace panties from her dresser along the way.

"Um, you want me to wait out here?" William hesitated at the threshold of her bedroom door.

"No way, I need answers." As William entered the inner sanctum of her bathroom, Julie turned her back, grabbed the hem of her nightgown and yanked it up over her head. With a quick twist of the handle in the shower, she turned back toward him, standing in just her I'm-at-work-and-don't-have-time-for-sex briefs. "Look, William, I need to know all the rules and I don't have time for modesty." To prove the point, she slipped her panties from her hips and stepped behind the shower curtain, a small smile tugging at her lips.

William's expression had been priceless. Based on the time lag since her request for answers, she'd guess her little show of skin had shocked the poor guy. Feeling a little on the guilty side since she had no intention of going to bed with the man, Julie relented. "Sorry. I should have been a little less forward."

The sound of William clearing his throat made Julie chuckle. "No problem," he said. "I don't miss an opportunity to see a beautiful naked woman, if I can help it."

"Thanks, William." With a handful of shampoo she scrubbed her hair with lightning speed. She could get used to this vampire speed thingy really quick.

"As to the answer to your questions, I already told you. The sun, wooden stakes and silver bullets are about all you have to worry about. Oh yeah and decapitation. Don't lose your head."

"Thanks, I'll try to keep that in mind." Ducking beneath the spray, she rinsed the soap from her head and made a quick run with the washrag over her entire body. She wanted to be clean and smelling fresh and feminine for her first night of sex with Roger. Speaking of which… "Should I call off my date with Roger?"

"Not unless you feel uncomfortable with your new…uh…status."

"But will he know? Will he guess? Should I tell him?"

"He won't know unless you step out in the sunlight and fry in front of him. Will he guess? I don't know the guy. Has he been with a vampire before?"

"How the hell should I know? I didn't know they existed until this morning." She yanked aside the shower curtain and pointed. "Will you hand me that towel behind you?"

"Uh, sure." William spun to grab the towel and toss it at her. His eyes were trained on the floor, but his gaze slipped upward to the juncture of her thighs and higher to her dripping breasts.

"Sorry." Julie couldn't help the little tingle of awareness coursing through her. What with the anticipation of fucking the cop, sex pretty much dominated her thoughts. Funny, she'd never considered William an object to lust after. Wrapping the towel around her middle, she tucked the edge in over her left breast and studied the man in front of her.

William was tall and thin, but he was well put together in a scholarly sort of way. Nice looking, brotherly type. But Julie only had eyes for her man in uniform.

She reached for her makeup and smoothed on a thin layer of foundation. "Why haven't you told me before now that you're a vampire?"

Leaning against the doorframe, William shrugged. "It's not something we like to advertise. It gets some folks upset and they think they have to kill us."

Like the not-so-psycho Bob Marley who was out there somewhere ready to kill every vampire he could lay his stake on. "Are there slayers, you know, like Buffy? I mean, can some people recognize a vamp on sight or smell?"

"Not usually. Although weres have a nose for them and can tell a human from a vamp."

Julie turned with her mascara wand in her hand. "Weres?"

"Werewolves, werecats, you know."

Her stomach plummeted to somewhere in the vicinity of her knees. "You mean there are such things as werewolves? Shit! Where have I been all my life?"

William took the wand from her hand. "Look up."

Standing like a frozen lump, she did as he said.

With the precision of an artist, William applied the black makeup to her eyelashes, careful not to poke her in the eye. "They live among humans, on the most part keeping their identity a secret. Occasionally a rogue vamp or were gets out of line, but we have security measures we initiate to bring them under control."

"Security measures?" she whispered, holding her face still to avoid being blinded.

"We dust the vamps and shoot the weres if they don't get a grip."

Julie grabbed his wrist and held the wand away from her eye. "You dust your own people?"

"Only the bad ones."

With a sigh, she leaned against the sink. "I think I should call Roger and tell him the date's off. I'm not ready for this."

The doorbell rang and Julie jumped.

William's lips twisted into a wry grin. "Too late, sweetheart."

"I'm not even dressed!" Julie ran for her closet. "Get the door, will you. I'll only be a minute." She stared at her closet full of clothes and moaned. "On second thought, I might be longer. I don't have a thing to wear."

"I'll let your man in."

"No wait!" She raced to block him from leaving her bedroom. "You can't. What will he think if he sees you in my apartment and me in nothing but a towel? I told him I live alone."

"What do you want me to do, disappear?" He shook his head. "Contrary to popular belief, vampires don't change into bats or disappear."

"Then get in the closet," she whispered, pushing him toward her clothes closet.

With a frown, he allowed her to maneuver him behind some of her long dresses. "Okay, this time. But make it quick."

"I will." She slammed the door shut as the doorbell rang for the second time.

Still wrapped in her towel, she sprinted across the living room and yanked open the door.

With Julie framed in the doorway with nothing but a towel between him and all her beautiful skin, Roger's mouth had no choice but to go completely dry. And he'd thought she was sexy in her nurse's uniform. Holy shit, she was hot. He cleared his throat and forced words past his lips. "Nice way to greet a guy."

"Get in here," she said, yanking him across the threshold. "I'm running a little behind."

"That's fine. Our reservation isn't until eight. Take your time. In fact…" He snagged her around the middle and pulled her into his arms. "We don't even have to go to the restaurant. We could call out for pizza or something and stay here." He nuzzled her neck and nipped at her earlobe. "Umm you smell like flowers. So what's it to be? Eat out or eat in?" Roger knew his preference and he tasted the main course by trailing kisses across her bare shoulder and downward to the edge of the towel.

Julie arched into him, sliding a naked leg up his chino-clad calf. "Tough decision," she muttered against the base of his throat where she pressed her lips and tongued the indention. Her leg climbed higher until she'd hooked it around his buttocks. With her arms circled around his neck, she wrapped the other leg around his waist and claimed his lips in a deep-throat kiss, he wasn't soon to forget.

The ride up his hips raised the towel, exposing her buttocks to his probing hands. Holding her steady, he carried her toward the bedroom, one goal in mind. To sink deep into her special wet place as fast as he could drop his zipper.

But when he crossed the threshold to her bedroom, Julie's hand shot out and caught the doorframe. "No!"

Her hold on the wood trim brought Roger to a jarring halt. "No? Was I just imagining your climb up my body?"

"I don't know what got into me." Her gaze darted around the room and to her closet. "Don't you think we're moving a little too fast?" She wiggled against him, her pussy rubbing the top of his waistband.

Roger groaned his frustration. His straining cock pressed hard against his zipper, begging for release from the confines of pants and briefs. After he'd gotten off work, he'd lain in bed wide-awake and unable to think of anything but Julie. Julie in her nurse's uniform, Julie sitting across from him at the restaurant. He'd even thought about fondling her beneath the tablecloth, teasing her into a frenzy before they finished their meal. He wanted her so badly he couldn't comprehend why she didn't want him as much. "You set the pace, baby." He kissed her lips and tried not to groan again as her legs dropped and she slid down his body, the towel rising higher.

Julie gave him a weak smile. "It'll only take me a minute to get dressed."

Roger reached out and tugged the towel over her hips. "I'll just wait in the living room." *Out of reach of your sexy body.* If his voice sounded a little disappointed, oh well. He'd have been perfectly happy to skip the meal and get right to dessert. With a glance at her rumpled bed, he forced himself to walk back into the other room.

"I'm really looking forward to the dinner at the Red Lantern tonight," she called out from the bedroom.

I'm looking forward to dessert. "I made the reservations as soon as I knew you and I were both off at the same time." He wanted to treat her to something special. She worked hard helping others and deserved a little pampering. Despite his driving desire to make love to her here and now, he could damn well wait and treat her with the respect she deserved. Since his divorce, Julie was the first woman he'd met that he felt he could trust. She deserved more than a quick wham-bam-thank-you-ma'am hop in the sack.

"Kim called a little while ago and said that psycho, Bob Marley, walked out of the hospital before morning."

"I should have taken him to the station." Then he might not have taken the call that ended with him and his partner being knocked on their cans.

"Any other excitement after you left the hospital?"

"Answered a call to a homicide."

"Really? Where?"

"About ten blocks from the hospital." Roger shook his head. "You need to be careful getting home at nights. The guy got away."

"Did you see him?" Julie peeked around the door, sliding a black spaghetti strap up over her shoulder.

"Yeah. The bastard was two or three inches taller than me and he had blond, spiked hair. His eyes were the most phenomenal red I've ever seen. He knocked me and my partner on our asses and took off."

She ran out to him wearing a short, black figure-hugging dress and no shoes. "Oh my God! Are you all right?"

He kinda liked it when she got all worried about him. He shrugged and pulled her against him. "Worried about me?"

"Yes, of course!" Her body shook beneath his

hands. "There are all kinds of monsters on the streets at night."

"I know. Just the reason I don't want you wandering around alone in the dark." He pulled her against him and rested his head against her cool damp hair.

She emitted a soft snort and said something under her breath that sounded like, "A little late for that."

"What did you say?" he asked.

"Nothing," she said, breezily as she danced away from him. "Just let me get into some shoes and I'm ready."

"I've been ready since I got here," he said beneath his breath, adjusting his trousers to ease the strain. How the hell he was going to get through the night without exploding first was quickly becoming a concern.

Julie dropped to her knees in front of her closet and dug around for shoes to match her dress.

"Wear these," William whispered, handing her a pair of black high-heeled sandals.

"I can't do this, William. I can't lie to him."

"Who said you have to lie?" William helped her to her feet. "Look, if it comes up in a discussion, tell him, otherwise, what he doesn't know won't hurt him."

"He has the right to know what I am."

"Are you sure this relationship is going somewhere?"

"It was." Tears swam in her eyes. "At least it was until I was turned."

"Then wait for the right moment. You don't want to scare him off on your first date."

"You're right. I don't want to scare him off on the first date." Julie sighed. "Hell, I almost jumped his bones a minute ago. I've wanted him so long, I can taste it."

"Uh, one more thing about being a vampire."

A frown settled between her brows and she could feel the beginning of a headache. "What? Isn't there enough?"

"Vampires have…shall we say…more intense appetites."

"I thought all we could eat was blood. Holy crap! The restaurant! What can I eat?"

"You can have a rare steak. That'll help tide you over until your first meal. If you wait until tomorrow night, I'll assist you. I know someone who can help us out."

"But I have to work!"

"Then we'll take care of it before you go on duty."

"Complicated. My life is too complicated."

"Uh, and Julie?"

"What else?"

"About the appetites?"

"Yeah?"

"They include sexual appetites. Be careful. Sometimes in satisfying his sexual appetites, a vampire can get carried away and satisfy his hunger as well."

Julie pressed a hand to her temple. "Is that why I was all over Roger?"

William nodded. "Afraid so."

"Great. Now I'm a bloodsucking nymphomaniac. Not something to write home to Mom about, is it?"

"Not unless your mother is very progressive minded."

"You okay in there?" Roger's voice sounded close to the door.

William disappeared behind the full-length gowns.

"Everything's fine. Found the right shoes. I guess I'm ready to go."

"Good, I thought I heard voices." Roger pushed the door open and smiled in at her. "You're not hiding a man in your closet are you?"

"No, of course not." Julie fought the blush creeping up her neck and grabbed her purse. "I talk to myself as I'm dressing. That's probably what you heard."

"Yeah. Ummm, you look good enough to eat." He pulled her into his arms and kissed her. "Sure you don't want to stay here and order out?"

"I'm sure, all right." She looped her arm through his and tugged him toward the door. "Come on. You're not getting out of taking me to a fancy restaurant. Afterward…well let's just say, I'll still be hungry."

Julie sliced into her steak, her pulse increasing as bright red juices squirted out onto the plate. Hunger, like a strong yearning, made her that much more aware of everyone around her. She caught herself staring at Roger's throat more than once and wondering what it felt like to bite into a vein full of warm, rich blood. Her gaze dropped to her plate and she stabbed a bite of meat. "Tell me something about you that I don't know." She popped the steak into her mouth and chewed. If she asked him all the questions, he might not have time to ask her the one question she dreaded most. *Are you a vampire?*

"I was married once."

Julie stopped in mid-chew and swallowed the lump of meat whole. "You were? As in past tense?"

He smiled and reached across to pat her knee.

Instead of calming her, the pat ignited adrenaline

in her system and primed her libido. Now she was hungry for sex as well as blood. How was she going to hold herself together without jumping Roger's bones in public?

With a serious frown creasing his forehead, Roger continued. "Unlike my ex-wife, I believe in the sanctity of marriage. I wouldn't be out with you if I were still married."

"Unlike your ex-wife?"

"Yeah, she slept around behind my back."

"Wow." Julie stared down at her plate. What did you say to something like that? Could you pass the pepper, please?

"Not that she has anything to do with us. I just thought you should know I'm divorced."

"I guess now is as good a time as any to know that."

He leaned toward her, concern written in his frown. "Does it change the way you feel about me?"

"No."

"Good." Roger sat back in his chair and rubbed the side of his face. "I'm glad we're together tonight. We haven't had time to really get to know each other. I feel like I've known you all my life, yet I don't know much about you at all."

"Not much to know," she said, dodging that bullet. "I'm a nurse, I live in Houston. I'm an only child and my parents live in Dallas." She shrugged. "That's about it."

"I see so much more to you." He took her hand in

his. "I can tell you love your job by the way you are with the patients and staff in the ER. You're warm, caring and beautiful. An angel of mercy."

Tears welled up in Julie's eyes and she pulled her hand free. "Thanks. I do love my job." But could she continue to work as a nurse now that she was a vampire? She stuffed the last bite of steak into her mouth and contemplated a confusing future.

"You have a little blood dripping from the side of your mouth." Roger reached across the table and dabbed at Julie's mouth with the edge of his napkin.

Her cheeks heated and she smiled up at him. "Sorry. I was just so hungry I couldn't see straight." She stared down at the bloody juice on her plate and wondered if she could get away with licking it dry?

"I like my steaks rare, but I think I would have sent yours back for an extra thirty seconds each side. Have you always eaten your steaks that rare?"

As she sat back in her chair, Julie lifted her own napkin to her lips. "No, but I will from now on. That was delicious and completely satisfying."

Roger leaned toward her. "Completely?" Beneath the tablecloth where their knees touched, Roger's hand slid across her thigh and up beneath the short hem of her black dress.

The steak had only whetted her "appetites" more and her knees fell open. "Not completely."

Scooting his chair closer, Roger's fingers tickled the inside of her thigh, inching toward the black lacy panties damp with juices that had nothing to do with rare steak.

If there weren't a hundred customers scattered around the busy restaurant, Julie would consider climbing onto the table and doing it there. The wicked gleam in Roger's eyes was enough to get her blood shooting through her veins at a remarkable speed, and the danger of getting caught doing naughty things beneath the classy table was enough of an attraction. She couldn't resist and opened her legs wider. Thank goodness for the long tablecloth.

He bent toward her ear and pressed a kiss to the side of her neck. "Ever come in a fancy restaurant?" At that exact moment, his finger traced the folds of her labia through the black lace of her thong bikini panties, barely skimming that ultrasensitive nub trapped between.

As she sank lower in her chair, Julie stifled a moan, her hand slipping beneath the pristine white table-cloth to join his. She guided him to the elastic edge of her panties and shoved his hand down over her mound of curls, her breath coming in short, ragged gasps. She was going to come all over the fine cush-ions of the straight-backed chairs if she didn't watch it.

"May I offer you something from the dessert menu?"

Roger smiled up at their waiter, all the while flicking her clit with his forefinger. "No, thank you. I think we have all the dessert we can handle."

Julie's tongue was glued to the top of her mouth and she closed her eyes so the waiter couldn't see them roll into the back of her head as she squelched the urge to squeal. *God, that felt sooo good!*

"Are you all right, madam?"

Her eyes popped open and she nodded. "Yes…yes. I'm perrrfect." Roger's finger dipped inside her and a smile climbed up her cheeks. "Thank you."

When the waiter walked away, Julie shot a teasing glare at Roger. "Now he's going to think I'm a nutcase." She started to push his hand away. "We shouldn't do this here. What if we get caught?"

His finger swirled around the opening of her pussy and upward to nudge against her clit. "Are you afraid?"

She thought for a moment, the adrenaline pulsing with the blood throughout her body. "No. And that feels so good."

"Then ride it."

"Here?" He hit her sweet spot and she practically jerked out of her chair. "Aren't you afraid you'll lose your job?" she said through gritted teeth.

"I like to live dangerously."

"Well, two can play that game." Her hand slid up his thigh and she cupped his package, squeezing firmly.

"Careful."

"Afraid?" He was hard as a stump beneath her fingers and his cock pulsed in her hand.

His lips tightened and he swallowed hard. "Maybe we should take this somewhere more—"

Julie squeezed again.

"Private," he ended on a gasp. His hand withdrew from her panties and he pushed back from the table, tossing his napkin on his plate. "Ready?"

With a smile teasing the corner of her lips, she straightened her dress and panties. "What? No dessert?"

"We'll go back to my place for dessert."

If they ended up at his place, she might not get back to hers before daylight. "Why don't we go to mine? I think I have some chocolate pudding and whipped cream in the fridge."

His brows climbed upward. "Do you always keep a stash of cream on hand?"

"For the right guest." She folded her napkin neatly and looked across the table at him. Should she tell him about her little problem before they did the nasty?

Roger ran his tongue across his bottom lip. "Ummm, whipped cream sounds tasty."

Okay, so maybe she'd wait to tell him after dessert. "Let's go." She jumped from her seat before he could help her with her chair. Her body was on fire and she couldn't wait to wrap her legs around him and fuck him until morning. Surely he wouldn't be mad when she told him about her condition. Maybe she'd tell him right after they had mind-blowing sex. As Roger lay in a comatose stupor of spent lust, Julie could whisper in his ear, "Oh by the way, you just fucked a vampire." These thoughts and many others raced through her mind as she headed for the exit. Delicious thoughts of how she'd eat her dessert were the most prevalent among the images. She'd tell him later—after the whipped cream.

Whipped cream. Roger trailed behind Julie distracted by her ass swaying beneath the clingy black dress with each step she took. He could imagine licking whipped cream from each rounded globe. "You should never have said anything about whipped cream," he muttered.

"But your face was priceless," she said, tossing her strawberry blonde hair over her pale, freckled shoulder. The thin strap on her left shoulder slipped down her arm.

Whipped cream on her shoulder would taste really good about now. Roger's cock twitched its agreement. "You're killing me here. And I thought you were sexy in your scrubs."

She stopped halfway across the restaurant floor and looked back at him over her bare shoulder. "Thanks. You're not so shabby yourself. What was it Kim said? Cop Candy? Umm…I love candy." Her tongue darted out and slid across her full, ripe lips.

"Cop candy, huh?" Roger grabbed her arm and hustled her between the tables. "You're tempting my sweet tooth. Let's go."

A disturbance at the entrance jerked Roger's attention from the woman next to him. A man pushed through the door, wide-eyed and hair sticking straight out.

"Hey, isn't that the nutcase I brought into the hospital last night?" Roger asked.

Julie stopped and stared at the man, her eyes wide in her pale face. "Y-yes. I believe you're right." She tugged at his arm. "Maybe we should go out the side door."

"I hope he doesn't plan on causing trouble. I'm off duty and I have better plans than writing up a report." His hand slipped down to cup her ass and squeeze. "Okay, make for the side door."

As Julie ducked toward the side exit, Roger glanced back at the self-proclaimed vampire slayer. The crazed man was staring right at him.

"Don't let her escape," Bob Marley screamed. "She's one of them!"

Roger stopped and glanced around at the people, staring across at Bob the psycho, regret building in his gut. "Great. I think I'm gonna have to go to work on my off time."

"No!" Julie grabbed his arm and pulled him toward the exit. "The restaurant has their own security handling it. See? You don't have to play cop 24/7. Let's go. That whipped cream is waiting."

"Stop that bloodsucking animal," Bob screamed across the room as two large men in black suits grabbed him by the arms and hauled him back toward the foyer.

As the bouncers dragged Bob away, whipped

cream crowded the gray matter in Roger's brain. "You're right. They seem to have it all under control. Let's get to that dessert."

Already at the side entrance, Julie didn't wait. She hurried through holding the door just long enough for Roger to make it through.

"What's the hurry?"

"I'm hungry," she said with a strained smile. "For dessert."

"We're parked around the back," he said, nudging her toward the rear of the building.

Weaving in and out of the row of cars, Julie pushed ahead. Damn, she was fast in high heels. Roger had to jog to keep up. What a woman. And she hadn't even broken a sweat. He could imagine those legs wrapped around him as he thrust deep inside. Was it hot outside, or what?

An early summer evening in Houston was guaranteed to be hot and humid, but the heat Roger felt was more than just the climate. "I wonder what delusion Bob Marley is living under? He looked like he was yelling at us as we left. Did you meet him last night?"

"Yeah, unfortunately." Her gaze darted around the parking lot as if searching for Bob. "Maybe he has it in for me for sticking him with a needle full of sedative."

"Did you happen to take any of his blood?"

"No, I didn't. But maybe one of the other nurses

did." She looked back at him, a frown creasing her brow. "Why?"

"He was screaming something about bloodsucking. I assumed you took blood. Otherwise, why would he say that?"

"Like you said, he's psycho. Who knows what goes on in a psychotic person's head? Where is your truck?"

"You're standing next to it."

"Oh, yes." She stopped and grinned. "So I am."

Roger closed the distance and pulled her into his arms. "Are you okay, Julie? You seem a bit distracted tonight."

She gave a combination between a laugh and a cough and laid a hand on his chest. "How could I not be distracted? I've been thinking about you and a night like this for as long as we've known each other."

"That would be two months, one week and three hours." He pulled her closer until the ridge of his fly pressed into her belly. "But who's counting?"

The anxious look in her eyes melted into a steamy emerald green pool of light reflected from the overhead streetlamps. "Don't forget the fourteen minutes and twenty-five seconds." Her hands crept up his chest and linked behind his neck, pulling him inescapably closer to her lips.

"I wouldn't dream of it." When their lips met, an explosion of desire ripped through him and he was pressing her against his SUV, his hands sliding over her shoulders and downward to cup her breasts.

She moaned beneath him, pressing into his cupped palms. One high-heeled foot slid up the back of his calf and her warm pussy rubbed against the top of his thigh.

A large hand, more like a vise grip, clamped onto his shoulder and jerked him backward and away from Julie. "What the f—"

The matching hand fisted and made a hard connection with Roger's stomach. The force of the blow sent him staggering, gasping for air.

The big Mack truck of a man was the same spiked-haired goon Roger had run into the night before. He snarled at him and then turned to Julie. "You're mine, now." Before Roger could catch his breath, the other man grabbed her arm and dragged her away.

"Like hell she is," Roger lunged after him and hit him with a football tackle, a technique that never failed to bring the bad guys down. Only this time, he might as well have hit a brick wall.

The man barely budged. He swept out a hand and swatted Roger to the side like a pesky fly.

Roger hit the pavement on his ass, his tailbone and his pride hurting with the impact. What did he have to do to bring him down? Roger considered himself in shape and fairly strong. He worked out every day of the week to ensure he was in top shape for his job with the Houston Police Department. Why wasn't his strength having any effect on this one man? He didn't know, but if he didn't hurry, Julie would disappear.

He crawled to his feet and took off after Julie.

Julie couldn't believe this was happening. The one night she was off at the same time as Roger and it was being completely ruined. Being turned to a vampire hadn't helped. Add to that, being singled out by a lunatic. To round out her date night, some big oaf of an idiot was dragging her away from the man she loved. Well, to hell with that!

"Let me go, you jerk!" Julie dug her high heels into the pavement and yanked her arm loose. "Who the hell do you think you are, busting up my date?"

"I'm Luke. Your master," he snarled, his lips lifting away from long incisor teeth that reminded Julie of a rabid wolf.

When she got a good look at him and his wicked fangs, fear gripped her. *Holy crap! This dude's a vampire!* Julie staggered back. Hadn't he said his name was Luke? She'd thought his blond hair and red eyes looked familiar. Kinda like the last face she saw before she'd been turned to a— "You!" As quickly as her shock faded, anger surged through her chest and she launched herself at him, doing what any self-righteous woman would do and dug her nails into that frightening face. "You son of a bitch! You did this to me! You made me—"

Luke grabbed her hands and flung her away like a dirty towel. "Stop, woman!"

Before Julie could spin around and attack again,

Roger stepped in front of her and faced Luke. "Leave her alone. Or I'll—"

"Or you'll what, human?" Luke lifted Roger by the collar of his shirt and hurled him to the side. "She's mine."

As Roger dropped to the ground, groaning, any fear Julie might have felt for her own safety disappeared. Her visions of a night of passion were quickly fading into her dreams, soon to be lost if she didn't do something to stop Luke. "Look, Bubba. You're not very bright are you? No one owns me. Got that?" She poked a finger at his chest like a child would poke at a hot iron. "I don't belong to anyone and I didn't ask for you to do what you did. So get lost before I lose my temper."

Tall-dangerous-and-dense snatched at her wrist and yanked her into his arms. "You belong to me."

"Like hell, I do!" Julie planted her hands against his chest and channeled all her anger and frustration into one mighty shove. After Roger's two attacks on the man, she didn't expect her little display of annoyance to have much impact.

But Luke flew backward and slammed against a car, his body hitting so hard, the metal crumpled behind him, leaving a butt-sized dent six inches deep in the door panel.

Julie pressed her hand against her mouth. *Holy crap! Did I do that?* She stared at her hands as if they belonged to someone else. William had mentioned she'd have speed, but he didn't say anything about strength. Roger hadn't been able to move the mountain of a vampire and she'd thrown him with nothing more than a little display of feminine PMS.

Roger.

She ran back to the man she'd been lusting after for days, sure he'd have a question or two after her little demonstration of testosterone-like strength. "Are you all right?" She extended a hand to help him up.

"I'm fine." He accepted her assistance, pulling himself to his feet. "But this guy isn't through with us." Roger straightened and reached for the pistol beneath his jacket, thankful he carried at all times. Luke was less than a yard from him when he unloaded five rounds directly into the man's heart.

"Bullets?" Luke laughed. "You're kidding, right?"

"That was five rounds." Roger glanced from his Glock to the man's chest where the bullets had entered. Other than the tears in his shirt, the blond-haired man didn't show any of the normal signs of mortal wounds like falling over and dying. "What's it take to kill you?"

"A lot more than bullets," Luke said. "On the other hand, I could snap you in two. So why don't you get out of my way?"

"No." Roger held his pistol out again. "Julie's my girl and you can't have her."

Almost melting at Roger's words, Julie had to pull herself together and think through the consequences of Roger's stand against a being at least twice as strong as him. "Uh, Roger?" Julie tapped Roger's shoulder. If he didn't move out of the way really quick-like, her evening of romance and sex was definitely going to be out of the question. Most likely, Roger would end up in the hospital with multiple fractures.

"Not now, Julie. I'm going to kick some major butt." He pushed his sleeves up his arms, a menacing scowl pushing his brows toward his nose.

"You?" The big guy's eyes widened. "You think you can take me?"

"Uh, Roger?" Julie tapped his shoulder again. "Luke isn't human. He could kill you."

"Not now, Jul—" He shot a glance her way. "What do you mean, he's not human? And how do you know his name?"

"He just told me his name is Luke. And believe me when I tell you he's not human," she repeated. "If you'll allow me...I'll explain later." She stepped around him and stood toe-to-toe with Luke. "Get lost, Luke."

The vampire bared all his teeth. "I'm not leaving without you."

"Then you'll be here a long time." Julie narrowed her eyes and gave Luke a determined look, hoping "that" look would make him back down and leave them alone. Otherwise, she'd be forced to kick his ass. "Get the truck, Roger."

"Not without you," he said, standing beside her.

"Think of your truck as a battering ram and just

do it. I'll be okay, really." She didn't look around to see if he complied. Certain her last attack had been dumb luck, Julie wasn't so sure she'd be able to hold Luke off for long. Surprise was her best weapon against an older vampire.

Here's to toppling the big guy. She ducked her shoulder and plowed into Luke's midsection, wondering if her best dress would be toast after she kicked the man's ass for ruining her date. Right now, she didn't care.

Luke flew backward into another vehicle as Roger's truck revved in the background. While the vampire struggled to pull himself together, Julie raced for the truck, yanking the door open and hopping in. She didn't breathe a sigh of relief until they were out of the parking lot and two blocks away from the restaurant.

Roger dug his cell phone from the clip on his belt. "I'm calling the department. That man needs to be apprehended before he hurts someone."

Julie shot a look in Roger's direction. If he called the police, they'd have to make a report of the incident. "I'm okay, you're okay. Let's call it even and go to my place."

"Are you crazy? The Houston P.D. needs to lock that guy up."

And what would they do to her if they discovered she was a vampire too? "Okay, but don't promise to go in until the morning. Unless the words 'whipped cream' don't mean anything to you anymore."

After a short call to the department, Roger pressed his foot to the accelerator. "I hope they catch him. I should have gone after him."

"How often do we have the same night off?" Julie slid across the bench seat and snuggled up to Roger. "I'm not letting some jackass ruin my evening with you."

His arm draped around her shoulders and he pulled her close. "No way. Whipped cream sounds good. And maybe some of that chocolate pudding."

Throw the dog a bone and he'll go after it. Julie smiled at her analogy, imagining doing it with Roger "doggie style". Hell, she'd do it standing on her head if he wanted to.

Now that the bad guy was long behind them, Julie could concentrate on Roger and making him want her just as much as she wanted him. And right at that moment, that was a lot.

Her hand slid up the lean muscles of his thigh to the ridge beneath his zipper. "Is it hot in here or is it just me?" Julie tugged at the low neckline of her dress and blew a stream of air down between her breasts.

Roger's glance dropped to the V of her cleavage. "It's definitely hot in here." When he looked up, he swerved to avoid hitting a stop sign. "Definitely hot in here," he muttered.

Julie sat up straight. "I'm sorry. I shouldn't do that while you're driving."

"No, you shouldn't if you want to get to your place in one piece." He drew in a shaky breath and blew it out. "And by the way. Where did you learn that linebacker move? When I hit that guy he didn't even budge. But you…" With a shake of his head. "What do they teach you in nursing school, anyway?"

"Oh, that?" Julie swallowed the wad of guilt lodged in her throat and forced a shrug. "I took a course in Tae Kwon Do once." She didn't volunteer that she'd quit when it came to sparring because she didn't want to hurt anyone. Funny how a little change like being turned to a vampire erased all her reservations about fighting. Or did she only want to fight the ugly nonhumans she didn't know existed before last night? Whatever. All she knew was that she could taste desire like a fine sip of wine swirling around on the back of her tongue and she had to clench her hands in her lap to keep them from straying back to Roger. If they didn't get to her apartment soon, she'd force Roger to stop on the side of the road for a little sexual snack to tide her over.

An innate sense of honesty niggled at Julie's conscience and surfaced. "Roger?"

"Um-hm?" Roger slowed to turn onto the street where she lived.

Don't tell him! Julie hesitated, her brain turning to whipped cream and chocolate pudding. "Oh, nothing." *Chicken!*

Roger pulled his truck up to the curb outside the old apartment house and shifted into park. Then he turned his beautiful and very sexy brown eyes toward her and smiled. "What's wrong, Julie? Having second thoughts? Because, if you are. I'll be fine—after a long cold shower—but I'll be fine."

"No way. I haven't changed my mind. It's just…" *I'm a vampire.* She couldn't make the words come out of her mouth and spoil the rest of an already crazy evening with the man she wanted to make love with.

"What, Julie?" He took her hands in his. "You can tell me anything."

CHAPTER 5

Julie's eyes widened and she stared up at him, her mouth poised to say something.

Roger held his breath. If she said she didn't want to make love with him, he'd die a thousand deaths before he could get to his house and that cold shower. His dick strained against the confines of his slacks and briefs, begging to be released.

After an excruciatingly long, drawn-out pause, Julie's eyes softened into a sexy droop and she smiled. "It's just…last one in gets the leftovers. I call dibs on the chocolate pudding!" She laughed out loud and grabbed for the door handle. Before he could reach out and kiss her, she was out of the truck and racing for the entrance to the apartment house.

A good two lengths behind, Roger chased after her, laughter bubbling up in his throat. Julie made him feel young and carefree. He loved that about the sexy, sassy nurse and wanted to be with her more often. She was helping to heal his wounds from his first marriage, and for that he would be forever grateful.

Gratitude wasn't what he had on his mind as they crossed the threshold of her apartment, clothes flying off before the door had time to latch behind them.

Julie reached down and slipped the strap from the back of her heels and kicked her sandals into a corner.

As Julie ran to the small kitchen, Roger unbuttoned the second button of his shirt, suddenly unsure of his role in the rest of the evening. One minute Julie has her hands in his lap, the next, she's hesitating over what to say. Despite her words to the contrary, was she having second thoughts?

With a squirt can of whipped cream and a two plastic cups of fat-free chocolate pudding, Julie rounded the corner of the fridge, smiling. "Choose your poison."

"I'll take the whipped cream. I like something I can point and aim."

"You're such a cop. Must be a guy thing to have something to point and shoot." She shot him a wicked grin and glanced at his crotch.

The look she gave him sent blood rocketing through his veins and the room grew increasingly hotter. He loosened another button on his shirt.

Her gaze followed the movement. "That's more like it."

"Are you going to keep that whipped cream or am I going to have to take it from you?" He reached for the can.

Instead of placing the can in his hand, Julie pressed the nozzle and squirted a small stream of the white fluffy concoction into his outstretched palm.

"Two can play that game." He scooped a finger full of the cream and drew a white line from the base of her throat down to the shadow of her cleavage.

Her eyes closed and she inhaled deeply. "Careful not to get it on my dress," she said, her voice like a breathy whisper.

"Let me take care of it," he traced another line of the white cream over her lips and down her chin to connect with the one at her throat.

She laughed a shaky, forced laugh, her eyes a pool of emerald green. "Pretty soon, I'll be covered with this stuff."

"Not if I have my way with you." He licked the rest of the cream from his hand, then gripped her shoulders and pulled her close enough to taste her sweet lips.

A bare calf climbed up the back of his leg and her arms lifted toward him.

"Uh-uh. Not yet." With his lips pressed to hers, he lapped at the cream and delved between her teeth, his tongue coating hers with the tasty treat. "Umm, good enough to eat."

When he pulled away to tackle the rest of the whipped cream, she followed him. Roger held up a finger. "We don't want to get cream on your dress, now do we?"

"To hell with the dress," she said and wrapped her arms around his neck, the can colliding with the plastic snack cups of pudding. She couldn't seem to get close enough

as waves of desire swept over her like a tsunami, engulfing her, consuming her and taking her to the darker side of lust. She couldn't stop the rising need any more than she could change what she'd become. If she didn't have Roger that night, she'd expire from a totally different type of starvation.

"Wait." Roger pushed her away.

"I can't wait." Dropping the can of cream and the tubs of pudding, she reached for his shirt and struggled with the buttons, too impatient to maneuver them out of the holes.

Roger laughed. "Let me, or I won't have any—"

Beyond caring, Julie grabbed each side of his shirt and ripped it open. Buttons popped off bouncing off her chest.

"Buttons left. Well, that's one way to do it."

What was wrong with her? She was destroying his clothes! Yet, she couldn't stop. Her fingers shoved the shirt over his broad shoulders and down his arms until the shirt fell to the floor. She reached behind him and cupped his ass, pulling him close enough the heat of his cock pressed into her belly.

"I didn't like that shirt anyway. It had whipped cream all over it." Roger cupped her face and kissed her long and hard. His lips broke free and he licked the cream from her chin, his tongue lapping at the trail down her neck to her breasts. He reached behind her and slid her zipper down the middle of her back.

Pushing the straps from her shoulders was all it took and the simple black sheath floated to a filmy puddle at her feet. The feathery stroke of the fabric ignited nerve endings all the way from her breasts to her toes. Naked except for the black lace thong, she stood ready for his next move. And if he didn't make it fast, she'd do it.

She wasn't disappointed when Roger's hands circled her waist and climbed upward to cup her breasts.

"Aren't you hot in all those clothes?" Was that her voice—that high-pitched, breathless sound? Her body was on fire and Roger stoked the furnace. "And where's that whipped cream and pudding?" She could use something to cool her off. What better way than chocolate pudding on her skin?

Roger flicked the button at his waist and unzipped his pants, his cock pushing outward, still encased in snowy white briefs.

Julie reached for him and skimmed her hand over the cotton fabric and down inside his trousers to cup his balls.

Grabbing her hands, Roger pulled her out of his pants. "How about I get the whipped cream and we take this in the bedroom?"

"Why waste time?" She tugged against his hands and he let go.

"Good point." He slipped off his shoes as Julie pushed his pants and briefs down his legs, dropping to her knees to complete the job.

From her position on the floor, Julie had a great view of Roger's magnificent penis. Free of clothing, he was wonderful to look at all over. His body was lean and muscular with dark hair sprinkled across his chest narrowing to a line down to the nest between his legs. She cupped his scrotum and massaged the sac between her fingers.

Groaning, Roger leaned his head back and breathed deeply, his fingers threading through her hair, tugging her mouth close to his cock. As enticing as his engorged cock was with the artery pulsing in his groin, inches from her teeth, Julie was torn between taking him full into her mouth and chomping into his groin. Her mind engaged enough to let her follow the more humanly correct urge. Opening her mouth wide, she wrapped her lips around him and pulled his hips forward until his penis bumped against the back of her throat.

Roger's hand fisted in her hair and he held her against him, his buttocks tight beneath her hands. Then he pulled her back by the hair. "I won't last four seconds at this rate. Give me the damned pudding." He pulled her up his body and kissed her,

then bent to retrieve the fallen can of whipped cream and plastic snack puddings. "Come on."

In a lusty haze, Julie let Roger lead her to the kitchen table where he lifted her to sit on the edge.

"I want my dessert," he said, with a strained smile.

"Well don't let me stop you." She took the chocolate pudding from his hand and peeled the foil top off. Then, dipping her finger into the smooth chocolate, she swirled it around. "Are you ready?"

He moaned. "You have no idea."

"Oh, I think I do." She painted the pudding around one of her nipples, tweaking it into a hard nub. With her newfound hyperactive sexual drive kicked into overdrive, she fought to keep from yanking Roger onto the table and having her way with him. If he wanted to pleasure her first, by all means, let him.

She dipped again and smoothed thick brown pudding over the other nipple, her eyes on Roger, not her handiwork.

The vein in his neck pulsed, pints of blood blasting through at an incredible pace.

Julie licked her lips and forced her gaze to return to Roger's.

He was watching her fingers teasing the other nipple.

"Your dessert is ready." She pointed her chocolaty finger at his mouth.

Like a hungry baby, he pulled her finger between his lips, sucking off the chocolate pudding. Once the creamy dessert was gone from her hand, his mouth laved first one then the other breast until all the pudding disappeared.

"All done?" Leaning back on her hands, Julie let her knees fall open.

"No way." Roger grabbed her ankles and planted her heels on the edge of the table. "I've only just begun." Lifting the whipped cream can, he pressed the nozzle between her folds, squirting out a hill of white cream.

The cool foam melted against her steaming clit, an exhilarating contrast to the heat he generated within her.

Roger dropped to one knee and lapped at the whipped cream. He parted her folds and tongued her clit until her ass squirmed against the smooth wooden table top.

"You're torturing me, Roger," she said and gasped as he hit her sweet spot, her insides tightening into an exquisite knot.

"Do you want me to stop?" He blew a tight stream of warm air against the moistness of her cunt.

Julie's heels dug into the tabletop and her bottom lifted upward. "No."

Using the pointed plastic tip of the whipped cream, Roger traced the folds of her labia, before he spread them wide and teased her clit with the jagged edge. His finger dug into her pussy, followed by two more, spreading her channel, widening her for more to come. He dragged the tip of the cream dispenser from her clit to the entrance to her vagina and pushed it lightly making a creamy mound of white foam over her entrance.

"Now for the crème de la crème of desserts." One leg at a time, Roger draped her thighs over his shoulders pulling her to the very edge of the table and into his mouth.

Her back arched and she cried out, "Roger! Jesus Christ, that feels so good."

His tongue dove in where his fingers had been, the whipped cream making it a long cool snake darting in and out of her. Rough hands gripped her ass and squeezed as he sucked the cream out of her.

The tension built to fever pitch and Julie felt herself losing control. When Roger touched his tongue to her clit, she spiraled over the edge and shattered into a billion powerful, surging pieces.

As she gave in to the orgasm, the change passed over her in a tide of shifting muscles. Even as the orgasm rocked her to the core, she was clawing at Roger, dragging

him up to a standing position. With whipped cream on his chin and his mouth shiny with her juices, he was the sexiest man she'd ever known. "I need you inside me now."

Wrapping her legs around his waist, she pulled him closer until his penis pressed to her opening.

That vein in his neck beckoned her and she fought the sudden urge to seal their lovemaking with her own special kiss. The frightening thought made her pull back, aghast at the direction of her desire.

She hadn't asked to be changed into a vampire. Hell, she hadn't known what happened until she almost baked in the morning sun.

Roger didn't deserve a life of the living dead. He should marry a nice young woman and make beautiful little baby boys who would grow up to look just like their daddy.

But that vein. Holy crap! It throbbed so enticingly.

"What's it to be? First you say you want me, then you push me away?"

"I can't."

"You're kidding right?" He pushed a hand through his hair.

"No, I'm not."

"Bring on the cool shower." Roger lowered her legs to the ground and pulled away from her dripping cunt.

No! She had to have him inside her. "Wait." She hopped off the table and turned her back to him, presenting her ass to him. The perfect solution to her bloodlust problem. "Fuck me, Roger—doggie style."

"Are you sure?"

"For Godsakes, fuck me!" She backed into his cock, the tip nudging into her anus.

Roger repositioned the velvety tip, touching the swollen nether lips of her vagina and this time, he hesitated. "What about birth control?"

"I can't have children. Will you do it already? I'm dying here." She rocked backward straining to take him fully into her.

His hands reached for her hips and he pressed her down onto him until he was fully sheathed. "I was thinking about how much I'd love to see your face while doing this."

Damn her and her bloodlust. "But this is fun, too, huh?"

His moan confirmed and he pistoned in and out of her, the friction building heat inside her.

Her fingers clawed at the table, the need to feed on fresh warm blood driving her system into a frenzy. How the hell did the vampires keep from sinking their teeth into their human lovers?

Roger's hand circled her hip and delved between her folds to find her clit. While rocking in and out of her, he rubbed his finger over that special place, raising her to climax at the same time as he slammed hard into her cunt.

He held her still, his rigid cock twitching within as his seed filled her.

Torrents of sensation rippled across her from her pussy outward, filling her with a deep satisfaction of having been thoroughly fucked. As the stirrings of lust subsided, so did her overwhelming need to feed. Julie collapsed against the table, sending a prayer of thanks to the vampire gods for the brief respite.

A very brief respite, she was soon to learn.

Roger had only just begun his assault on her body and senses.

CHAPTER 6

A tingling sensation not unlike that of a million needles prickled the skin of Roger's right arm. When he tried to move it, a soft moan sounded next to him. His eyes opened, the fog of sleep lifting like early morning clouds burning off in the sunlight. Strawberry blonde hair tickled his chin and he turned to discover the source of the tingles and tickles.

Julie lay in the crook of his arm, her face turned toward his chest, her blonde eyelashes lying against pale cheeks.

Roger's heart swelled, making his chest tighten. He and Julie had finally had a night together and it had been everything he'd hoped for and more—if he glossed over the initial distractions of a couple crazy men at the restaurant. Unlike most of his sexual relationships since his divorce, Roger didn't have even the slightest urge to jump out of bed and run from this woman. Although his arm had fallen asleep under the pressure of her head, he'd rather have this quiet moment to observe her while she slept.

Her long burnished golden hair spread out across his shoulder and onto the pale blue rumpled sheets. She looked like an angel, so soft and sweet in the morning. Roger glanced at his watch on the night-stand—make that afternoon light.

She shifted and nuzzled her nose against his chest, one eye easing open.

"Good afternoon, beautiful." He kissed her fore-head, the simple gesture reminding him of a more passionate version explored throughout the night. The reminder ignited less simple reflexes in his groin.

"Afternoon?" Rolling off his arm, she turned toward her alarm clock. "It is, isn't it? I have to go to work in a couple hours."

"Me too." Now that his arm was free, he shook the blood back into it. "Hungry?"

With a groan, she flopped back onto the pillow beside him, her eyes closed. "Ummm, yes. But not for food." She tossed the sheets aside and rolled on top of him, straddling his hips. "I had something a little more interesting in mind for breakfast."

The twin mounds of her ass rested over his rapidly swelling cock and the warmth only added to the heat building inside. "I think I could find the can of whipped cream."

"No need. I'll provide all the cream you want." To

prove the point, she slid lower until her cunt rubbed across the hard ridge of his penis, spreading a thin coating of cream along its length.

He nudged the entrance to her pussy with the tip of his cock. "I get your point."

"As I get yours." She reached behind her to fondle his balls and then positioned his cock, ready for mounting.

"What a woman." Roger cupped his hands behind his head and smiled up at her. "This is the kind of service I like. I just lie back and enjoy the view and action. You do all the work."

Instead of sliding down over him, she climbed off him and reversed her direction. "Give a little to get a little, mister."

She presented her ass toward him, planting a knee on either side of his ears, widening her legs until her pussy hovered over his lips.

He slapped her ass. "Are you always this bossy in the morn—afternoon?" He stretched his tongue out and tasted her juices. "Mmmm. Sweet, just like you."

"I'm anything but sweet," she said as her lips closed over his cock.

Surging upward, he filled her mouth. He palmed her butt cheeks, easing her lower so that he could treat her to the same bliss. Once she was positioned where he wanted her, he spread her folds wide and laved her clit, sucking it into his mouth, his tongue flicking a light, steady rhythm similar to the in-and-out motion she performed on his cock.

His hands smoothed across her buttocks, finding the crease and sliding down the center. When he found the tightly puckered lips of her anus, he circled it several times, lightly fingering the opening.

Her legs quivered and her pussy creamed.

Satisfied he wasn't entering taboo territory, he plunged his forefinger inside her ass at the same time as he delved his tongue into her pussy.

Julie's back arched and her mouth left his penis. "Ahhhh." Her head dropped to his groin and she leaned into his finger.

Cool air hit his wet cock at the same time as Julie nipped at his groin.

He jerked and cried out, "Ouch! The woman has fangs."

The nipping stopped and Julie stared at where she'd bit. "I'm sorry."

"I was kidding. I'll live."

She stared at his groin for a moment longer, then she flung her hair to the side and bent to the task of sucking his cock again. Her asshole gripped his finger with each time he forced it in and out.

He concentrated his assault on her clit, sliding his tongue over the swollen nub, flicking and nipping.

The combination of finger-fucking her ass and stroking her clit had her quivering from head to toe. Her mouth worked fast and furious over his penis, her fingers gently massaging his balls.

As his body tensed and his butt muscles clenched,

hers jerked to a stop, her mouth opening to emit a squeal around the thickness of his dick.

He flicked her faster until she scooted her pussy up and out of his range. Then she went to work on him, coaxing him to the peak and over the top, his body going rigid with his orgasm.

Cum surged up and outward in a sporadic gush. He tried to pull free of her mouth, but she followed him, swallowing his juices. When she pulled free, she licked his cock,

the long, tender strokes easing the tension from him until he fell back against the bed, breathing hard.

Roger drew in a deep breath and blew it out. "That was incredible."

"You're telling me?" Julie tipped over and flopped to the side of him, staring up at the ceiling. "I don't know if I could handle that on a regular basis. On second thought, yes, I could." She reached out a hand and smoothed it over his groin, her fingers tangling in his hair. Her legs lay open, inviting.

Rather than being drained by his recent orgasm, Roger was energized and ready to go at it again. He rolled off the bed and pulled her legs to the edge. "Now, get ready to be fucked."

Julie closed her eyes, telling herself she could handle this better without looking at his throat and the pulse, filled with hot red blood, beating just beneath the skin. She'd almost fed off him when her mouth encountered his groin. Her teeth had broken the skin, drawing a drop of blood. If he hadn't cried out, she'd have sunk deeper and fed off him. Why couldn't she control her urges?

She lay with her knees pushed up to her armpits, her eyes squeezed shut to the tempting source of nourishment.

Roger pressed the velvety tip of his penis to her entrance. "Look at me, Julie."

Oh please, don't ask me to do it. She opened one eye and tried not to stare at his neck.

"I want to see your pretty green eyes as I drive my cock into you."

"And I want you to shut up and fuck me." Her eyes widened at her frank language. Before last night, she'd reserved the F-word for the occasional rude driver and then only on rare occasions. Her actions had been less than normal since her turning. Would she change completely? Would the old Julie be replaced by the brash and sexually insatiable new Julie? If so, bring her on! Julie raised her legs and wrapped them around

Roger's waist. Careful to regulate the amount of pressure, she slammed him into her body until his cock stretched and filled her channel. "Ummm, that's more like it."

One corner of his mouth pulled upward. "Mind if I do some of the work? I believe in equal opportunity, but I'd really like control this time."

"So long as you get down to business and quit teasing me."

"One night in bed and she's a tyrant." His smile

softened his words and he leaned over her, to take a nipple between his teeth. "I like these just as well without the whipped cream." He slid in and out of her in a slow, gentle rhythm.

"I'll have to stock up on whipped cream and chocolate pudding." Julie released the grip she had on his waist and pulled her knees back to her armpits for maximum penetration.

"And I'll have to stock up on vitamins to keep up with you." The rhythm increased until he pounded in an out of her. A sheen of sweat glowed over his muscular body, highlighting that damned vein in his neck.

Julie closed her eyes and bit into her lip, willing the bloodlust to abate as her own sexual desire mounted. If she wanted to date Roger, she had to control her hungers.

Roger rocked to a stop, his head thrown back, his teeth bared as he came inside her. When his penis stopped jerking against the walls of her vagina, Roger scooted her up onto the bed, carefully maintaining their intimate connection. Then he collapsed on top of her rolling them both onto their sides, his neck within easy biting range.

What? Is he just trying to drive me crazy? Her stomach rumbled.

Roger chuckled, nuzzling her neck. "Hungry?"

"Yes, but I need to start getting ready for work and I have an errand to run before I go."

He leaned up on his elbow and looked down at

her. "Sounds like you're trying to brush me off?" His finger trailed over her nearest breast and down to her bellybutton.

"I wish I didn't have to go to work tonight." She gazed into his deep brown eyes. "How soon until we get another night off together?"

His hand cupped her furry mound. "I'm off tomorrow night."

Julie almost jumped off the bed. "Me too!" Then she fell back to earth. "That is, if you'd like, we can have dinner here."

His finger dipped into her cunt. "And dessert?"

"Like I said, I'll stock up on whipped cream."

$$\sim$$

"OKAY, GIRLFRIEND, SPILL." Kim stood in front of the ER nurses station, hands on hips, her white, rubber-soled shoes tapping noiselessly against the polished linoleum tiles. "You've been walking around the hospital like a zombie all night. Did your date go sour last night, or what?"

"What can I say?" Julie had slinked around the hospital ER, her head downcast, her normally happy smile squashed behind tight lips. Every time she saw blood or stared too long at a person's neck, she salivated. Her shoulders were so tense it would take a master masseuse to work out the kinks. She'd avoided everyone since she'd gotten to work, looking for excuses not to be alone with anyone, especially

Kim. She couldn't tell Roger what had happened to her last night, why did she think she could tell her best friend? Not to mention, her fangs were beginning to show.

Kim's foot stopped tapping. "You two did get some action, didn't you?"

Her face flaming, Julie glanced around before hissing, "Of course we did."

"Then what's the problem? You've been sneaking around here like you're afraid to talk to anyone. If you can't talk to me, who can you talk to?"

Julie sighed. If she didn't tell someone, she'd explode. "Come on." She grabbed Kim's arm and hurried her to the janitor's closet.

Kim giggled as Julie shoved her inside and shut the door behind her. "Are we going to have a little girl-on-girl time? Cause if we are, cool. I've always wanted to experiment." She reached for one of Julie's breasts.

Julie leaped back, banging into a wire shelf of toilet paper, slapping at Kim's hand. "No!"

Her lips twisting in a disappointed grin, Kim crossed her arms over her chest. "Well, hell. Go ahead and tell me your deep dark secret before Lindeman finds us."

Taking a deep breath, Julie launched into the digest version of what happened since the last time she'd been at work, leaving out her night of passion with Roger. When she finished, she leaned back and studied her friend's face.

For a long moment, Kim stood with her mouth unhinged and then her lips spread into a wide grin. "That's so cool! You mean you're a real honest-to-God vampire?" She reached out and lifted one of Julie's lips, her thumb grazing the tip of a fang. "Wow! Check out the hardware."

With a frown, Julie slapped Kim's hand away. "It's not cool. It changes everything."

"What did Roger have to say?"

Julie stared at the floor. "He doesn't know."

"You didn't tell him?"

"Don't you see? I didn't want to spoil our first night together." She didn't regret the incredible sex, but she knew she should have told him and let him make an informed decision on whether or not he wanted to fuck a vampire.

"You know about Roger's ex-wife, don't you?"

"Yeah, apparently she screwed around on him. So?"

Kim rolled her eyes. "So, Roger has trust issues. By not telling him as soon as you found out, you may have created a huge problem."

"How so?"

"You're kidding me right?" Kim grabbed Julie's shoulders and stared her in the eye. "You've lied by omission. If, or rather when, he finds out, he's likely to go ballistic."

Her empty stomach dropped to her knees and all her happy dreams about her next meeting with Roger disintegrated. "Fuck."

Kim hugged her and gave her a fake smile. "Then again, maybe he won't notice."

"Not notice these?" Julie peeled back her lips, exposing her fangs.

"Okay, so you're a little different now." Kim pushed her long, straight black hair out of her eyes. "You gonna let a couple of funky teeth come between you and the man you love?"

"It's not just the teeth. There's the blood drinking, scorching in the sun, crazy vampires claiming to own me and a slayer out to stake me at every turn."

"So, you have a few other challenges." Kim shrugged. "You're a tough lady. Deal with it."

"A few challenges?"

"Main thing is that you have to tell Roger."

"I know." Julie's shoulders sagged. "But how?

"Tell him the next time you see him."

"What if he comes to the hospital?"

"Okay, so maybe the next time you two are alone."

Her stomach knotted at the thought, but she knew she couldn't keep the knowledge from him, if they were to have any kind of lasting relationship. "Okay. Tomorrow night I'll tell him."

A shout sounded out in the hall, followed by more yelling.

"What the hell?" Julie jerked the door open.

Nurses and orderlies ran away from the entrance.

Head Nurse Lindeman raced the opposite direction yelling, "Call security, now!"

At the entrance to the emergency room Bob

Marley stood with a loaded crossbow. When he saw Julie, his eyes flared. "There she is!" He raised the crossbow and aimed it at Julie. "She's the devil and must be purged from the earth."

Instinct kicked in and Julie dove into Kim, knocking her to the ground, just as a wooden arrow hit the supply closet door. Had they stood still, one of them would have been the recipient of that arrow.

Two security guards showed up as Bob Marley was loading the next arrow into the crossbow. They tackled him and took away his crossbow.

Bob shouted throughout the ordeal. "But she's the devil's spawn! She'll turn you all or kill you. Mark my words!" He was still shouting when Lindeman stuck him in the ass with a heavy dose of sedative.

As his words slurred and finally trailed off, the entire ER staff loosened up. Some laughed, others stared at Kim and Julie and shook their heads.

Lindeman strode by, her demeanor no different than any other day in the hospital. As if crazy men wielding crossbows was a normal occurrence.

Julie admired the woman more each day. She stood by as they carried Bob Marley to an examination room, a chill crawling across her skin.

"You think he knows?" Kim asked in a whisper.

With a snort, Julie brushed at her scrubs. "I'd bet my last dollar he knows what I am."

Just when Julie thought the night couldn't get worse, Roger entered the ER with his partner, Chase. He rushed to Julie, his face creased in a worried frown. "I heard what happened from one of the EMTs as I came in. Are you all right?"

"I'm fine." He looked as good as an ice cream sundae on a hot day. Julie practically drooled all over his dark blue uniform.

Roger's mouth thinned into a straight line. "We'll take care of Marley so he doesn't bother you anymore."

"You won't hurt him, will you?" After all the man was right. She was a vampire and he was only trying to rid the earth of the bloodsucking creatures. He meant well for mankind, even if it involved genocide of a bunch of living dead people. Julie couldn't help but feeling a little sorry for Marley.

"No, sweet Julie." He lifted a hand to cup her face, smiling down at her with a loving glint in his gaze. "We won't hurt him. But we'll lock him up in a padded cell."

Julie wanted to run and hide from the truth. Roger was too good for her. Instead, she turned her face into his palm and kissed it. "Thanks."

"Are we still on for tomorrow?"

"Eh-hem." Kim stirred beside her.

Julie jammed her elbow into Kim's side. "Yes. And, Roger, we need to talk." She shot a glare at Kim as if to say, *Are you satisfied?*

Before Roger could respond another shout rang out.

One of the security guards raced in from outside.

"Get a gurney out here. Out in the alley behind the hospital. We have a man down."

The trained professionals raced to respond. Julie set off at a run toward the exit, Roger close behind her.

"Over here." The security waved from the alley. "I think he's dead."

Roger sprinted ahead of the gurney, nurses and orderlies, his gun drawn. "Stay back until I clear the scene."

The security guard unhooked the safety strap from his holster and drew his weapon.

Julie cringed. He probably hadn't drawn that weapon for all of the ten years he'd worked there.

Roger ducked into the alley and back out. "It's clear, but the guard's right, this man's dead."

Orderlies lifted the victim onto the gurney and transported him into the hospital. Once inside, nurses and the doctor on duty gathered around, checking for any traces of vital signs. The man was cold, so he'd been dead long enough reviving wasn't an option.

Kim stood by the man's head, her face paler than the white makeup she used in her Goth persona. She stared across his chest at Julie then pointed at the twin puncture marks on the man's neck.

No signs of blood were evident on his lips.

Julie wanted to sink through the floor.

Fuck. She'd bet her last dollar the stiff was a couple pints low on blood.

CHAPTER 7

Roger stuck around the hospital and talked to as many of the staff as he could who might have been outside at the time of death, guesstimated to be less than a half-hour earlier. By the time he finished interviewing people in and around the hospital, it was two-fifteen in the morning and he was on duty until five. Tonight was going to be a long one.

An hour into the interviews, he cornered Julie. "I don't want you leaving this hospital without an escort to your car. That's the second murder with the same M.O. in the past three nights."

She held up her hand scout-style. "Trust me. I'm calling security before I cut out of here."

"These murders are unusual and I don't like it. Who goes around draining the blood of their victims in alleys?"

Julie shrugged. "You got me."

He smiled. "And I'll see you tonight?"

"Can't wait." Her response seemed less than enthusiastic.

"Something wrong?" he asked.

She looked toward the exit, refusing to meet his eyes. "I'd say two murders are enough to have anyone worried."

He grabbed her hand and tugged on it. "That's not what I meant. Is there something wrong between us?"

She glanced at where their fingers entwined. "Why do you ask?"

"I don't know. You seem different somehow."

A soft snort escaped her lips. "You're telling me." She looked into his eyes. "Just promise me we'll talk later."

His gut knotting, Roger replied, "You bet." What could be so dire that Julie wouldn't look him in the eye? And she hadn't smiled at him once since he'd arrived at the hospital. He leaned forward and kissed her. "I have to collect my prisoner from the psych ward before I leave. Maybe I'll see you on my way out?"

"That would be great." Her lips curled upward, but her lips didn't part into her normal full grin.

Roger had a bad feeling about her responses. Thank goodness they were meeting later. The more he'd been around Julie, the more he realized she was the girl for him. Usually, she was happy and smiling, a joy to be around and full of fun and laughter. His ex-wife had always complained about one thing or another, usually to do with him. Not Julie. Whatever was troubling her could be worked through. Together.

He liked the ring of that. For two years, he'd been just Roger. Not part of a couple and no desire to ever go that route again. Julie had changed all that and he wasn't giving up on her without a fight.

As he passed the rooms along the hallway, he planned his methods of seduction for the night ahead. He couldn't wait to try out the flavored whipped cream he'd found at the market.

Chase met him outside the door of Bob Marley's room with a wheelchair. "You ready for this one?"

Roger shook his head. "Not really. But we'd better get him out of the hospital before he causes any more damage."

"Still hard to believe the man shot a crossbow in the hospital, at your girlfriend, no less."

Roger fought the surge of anger. If he'd been there when Marley shot at Julie, he'd have killed the man. The nut was lucky Roger had had time to cool off. He pushed through the swinging door into the room.

Bob Marley lay stretched out on a gurney, his arms strapped to his sides, an IV pumping sedatives into his veins. But he was awake. "Gotta cleanse the earth," he muttered his words slurred like he'd had one too many.

"You aren't cleansing anything tonight, but the inside of a jail cell."

"Can't do that. They're all over the city. Must warn." He tugged against the restraints.

Chase pulled handcuffs out of the case attached to his belt and clipped them on Marley's wrists before unbuckling the restraints. "You have one call from the police station. You can call your lawyer and warn him."

Chase and Roger hauled Bob Marley off the gurney and settled him into the wheelchair. As they rolled him out of the room, Julie and Kim passed by.

"She's one of them." Marley lunged from the wheelchair and fell flat on his face. He struggled to get his cuffed hands beneath him and pushed to his knees.

The two nurses hurried around the corner, out of sight.

"Gotta stop them. They'll take over the entire city." Bob swayed toward Roger. "Don't you see? You're a cop, do something."

"Not in this life, buddy." Roger waved toward the chair. "Take a seat, sir."

"Oh, I get it, you're in on it with them." Bob lunged at Roger's face.

Unprepared for the attack, Roger blocked the man's hands.

"Vampire lover!" Marley yelled. "God will strike you down!"

Roger and Chase wrestled the man back into his seat and cuffed him to the arm of the wheelchair.

When they had him subdued, Chase chuckled. "So

how does it feel to be a part of a vampire conspiracy?"

"Don't encourage him."

"That's what it is," Marley said. "A conspiracy to take over the city."

"Yeah and the ER nurses are vampires." Roger shook his head.

Standing in the side hallway leading to the radiology lab, Julie hovered, waiting for Marley to leave the hospital. She'd heard everything.

Kim appeared. "You can come out now. They're gone."

Julie stomped down the hall. "Jesus! Doesn't that guy ever give up?"

"What I don't get is how he can tell you're a vampire." Kim hurried to keep Julie's angry pace.

"Maybe he is some kind of special vampire hunter. I need to talk to William. That's just one of the questions I have for that guy." She glanced at her wristwatch. "I get off in ten minutes. You're on the same shift tonight aren't you?"

"Yeah," Kim replied.

"Could you give me a lift home?"

"Sure. If you promise me I get to meet your male vampire friend." Kim's eyes glowed. "Wow, I've never met a real male vampire before."

"Hunh," Julie grunted. "From what I understand, you probably have and don't even realize it."

"Wow. That's just too cool."

As Julie and Kim walked back toward the nurses

station, Kim stared at everyone walking by as if trying to determine if any of the patients or staff were vampires. She studied some people so long, she made them frown.

Julie grabbed her arm. "Stop it or they'll be sedating you next."

The drive back to the apartment building was blissfully uneventful. Instead of going straight to her apartment, Julie knocked on the door across the hall. "Please be in."

William opened the door with a smile, and his fangs weren't showing.

"That's my first question." Julie shoved him through the door, Kim on her heels. "Kim's a friend from work. She's human and she knows what we are."

"Nice introduction." William held out his hand to Kim. "William Fagan and you are?"

"Yours." Kim all but drooled all over William. "I mean, my name is Kim Erikson."

"Enchanted." William bent to kiss her knuckles, holding her hand longer than necessary.

Julie couldn't remember William kissing her hand for that long when they'd first met. "If you'll pick your jaw off the floor, Kim, I need this guy for a few." Julie broke Kim's handhold on William.

Twin flags of color lit her friend's pale cheeks and she glanced away. "Of course. Don't mind me. I'll be as quiet as a mouse."

William turned his attention to Julie. "What was it

you wanted?"

"Answers." Julie paced across the floor and back. "First." She opened her mouth and pointed to the extended incisors. "If you're a vampire, why don't yours show?"

"They retract." William bared his teeth and extended his fangs. After a few seconds, they receded into his gums. "Next question."

"How did you do that?" Julie moved closer to stare into the vampire's mouth.

"Yes, how do you do that?" Kim crowded closer as well.

"It comes natural. You think about feeding and your fangs extend. New vampires take a day or two to get used to them."

"Why didn't you tell me that last night while I fed on that pint of blood you brought me?"

He shrugged. "I didn't think to. I've been doing it for over two hundred years. After that much time, you tend to forget the nuances."

"You're over two hundred years old?" Kim touched William's arm. "You don't look a day over twenty-nine."

Was that a blush rising in William's cheeks? "Thank you."

"Excuse me? You mean to tell me I suffered all night on duty refusing to smile because of these damned fangs, and I could have retracted them?"

"Were you thinking about feeding all night?"

"Thinking about it?" Julie threw her hands in the

air. "I was freakin' obsessed! Everywhere I turned there was blood."

"Kinda comes with the ER territory." Kim smiled at William. "I'm a nurse."

"An angel of mercy."

"Could you two cut the mush long enough for me to get answers to my questions?" Julie cast a glance to the ceiling and prayed for patience. "There's a guy called Bob Marley who swears he's a vampire hunter."

"I've heard of him."

"He knows I'm a vampire. How? Can vampire hunters sniff us out or something? I sure didn't tell him I was of the fanged variety. He found me at the restaurant, turned up at the hospital and took a shot at me with a crossbow." Julie took a deep breath. "How does he know?"

"Calm down and let me research." William pulled a worn leather-bound book from a shelf and flipped pages. "Does he have a tattoo on his neck?"

William's seriousness was new to Julie. She's always seen him as the nice guy next door, nothing more. This knowledgeable vampire had been hiding behind his retractable fangs all along. Kim seemed to notice everything about him from the get-go and she appeared to be completely smitten.

"I didn't get a chance to look at the back of his neck," Julie said.

"Oh, I did!" Kim the Goth, supercool chick, jumped up and down like the spring-butt everyone hated in school. "There was this blue crucifix symbol on the back of his neck, it started at the base of his skull and went down his neck to his shoulders."

William held the book open to an ink drawing of an elaborate crucifix with scrolled edges and intricate embellishments.

Kim went so far as to squeal. "That's it!"

William turned to face Julie. "We've got problems."

"You're telling me," Julie muttered.

"Seriously, listen to him, Julie." Kim ran her finger across the page. "These guys are relentless."

"She's right. They're from a long line of vampire hunters, raised to believe vampires are evil."

Julie snorted. "That's ridiculous. I'm not any more evil now than before I was a vampire." Memories of her intense sexual urges and the desire to bite surfaced. "Am I?"

"No, of course not. We can lead normal lives like any human, with the few limitations I outlined."

"The daylight thing and the need to feed on blood."

"Exactly. We do have a more heightened libido and bloodlust can be a concern. But with a little restraint, vampires are no different than humans."

"Oh yeah?" Julie planted her fist on her hips. "What about Luke Hester?"

William snapped the book shut and replaced it on the shelf. "Compare him to a sociopath. He's mentally out of control. Not all vampires are like him."

"Yeah, but when you can hurl a man across a parking lot, that makes you a lot more dangerous than a mere mortal."

"Yes, but he's no more evil than a serial killer."

"Good point. Then why can't we convince Mr. Marley we're the good guys?"

"He's been brainwashed all his life to believe it's his sacred duty to cleanse the earth of vampires."

Kim gripped William's arm. "That's just what he said before he tried to shoot Julie with the crossbow."

William only nodded, his gaze catching Julie's.

"Great." She flung her hands in the air. "I have a lovesick vampire claiming he owns me and a vampire hunter trying to kill me. Not to mention, I need to tell my boyfriend he made love to a vampire last night." Julie walked to the window and stared out into the gray light of predawn. "I'm not usually a whiner, but I'm feeling a bit overwhelmed."

William moved to stand behind her and placed a hand on her shoulder. "You're a strong woman, I'm sure you will persevere."

"I hope so. As long as Marley doesn't dust me or Luke doesn't haul me off to his secret lair." She shivered at the thought of being with the crazed psychopath. The she straightened her shoulders and turned to face William and Kim. "First things first. Roger needs to know what he's up against with Luke and Bob. If he doesn't already know about vampires, tonight he gets a lesson in Vampire 101."

CHAPTER 8

Roger arrived five minutes late for his date with Julie. All the way over in his SUV, his mind churned. He couldn't believe what he'd just heard at the police station.

When Julie answered the door, he pulled her in his arms and kissed her hard on the lips.

Her hands slid up around his neck and she deepened the kiss, her teeth parting to allow his tongue access to hers.

The kiss turned to heavy groping with Roger's hands finding their way beneath Julie's shirt. He wouldn't have stopped there if not for a loud throat-clearing sound.

"Do you mind?" a voice said behind him.

Julie backed up a step, her face flaming. "Oh, hi William, this is Roger."

"I hope so. I'd hate to think you were attacking a

perfect stranger." William held out a hand. "William Fagan."

"Roger Decker. I'd shake your hand, but I'm otherwise occupied." He resented the other man's intrusion and he didn't want to stand in the hallway talking to him when he could have Julie all to himself. "If you'll excuse me, I need to talk to her." Roger hustled Julie through the door, his hands still beneath her shirt. After he kicked the door shut behind him, he leaned forward to kiss her again.

Julie held a hand up to his mouth. "Wait."

"Wait?" All he wanted to do was kiss her, as if by kissing her, all the things he'd heard in the station briefing that afternoon would go away.

Unfortunately, she was firm. "Yes, we need to talk."

Of course. He had to tell her what he'd heard. Let her know of the present threat to the city. "You're right. I need to tell you what's been going on."

"You need to tell me?" Her brow wrinkled. "Tell me what?"

"No, ladies first."

Julie stepped back another step until Roger's hands dropped from her waist. She wrapped her arms around herself. "Mine can wait. Yours sounds more important."

"Okay." Roger pushed a hand through his hair and stared into the far corner. "Whew. How do I say this?"

"I'm not liking it already." She rubbed her arms as though she felt chilled.

"Just wait. You're not going to believe this."

"Then tell me."

"The chief called every policeman in from off duty for a big debrief on what's been going on with all the murders lately."

Her eyes narrowed. "Yes. Go on."

"You really aren't going to believe this."

Julie scowled and stomped her foot. "Tell me already."

"Okay, okay. He told us that Houston has been invaded by vampires. That's who's been killing all those people." He stopped, his brows raised. He'd expected her to laugh him out of her apartment. When she didn't, it was his turn to scowl. "You don't look shocked by the news."

"I'm not."

"But the chief said *vampires*." Roger couldn't believe how well she maintained a straight face. Was she just a really good actress, or what? "Aren't you afraid our police chief has gone off the deep end?"

Julie shrugged, but didn't respond.

"I thought it was a big hoax until they showed us the evidence. Every victim, and there have been eight so far in the past two weeks, had two puncture wounds somewhere on their bodies. Most of them were on the neck."

"Go on."

"I thought it was someone's idea of a big joke, but

then they brought in a couple of plainclothes policemen who'd been out on the beat when one of the attacks occurred. They gave the same description as our guy from the restaurant parking lot."

"They did?" Again, her reaction was little more than lukewarm.

"Yeah. That's when I started listening. He attacked them too and they confirmed what we already knew. He's got superhuman strength and bullets didn't faze him."

"Damn." Julie's face paled. "Our friend Luke gets around."

An uneasy feeling crept through Roger. Something wasn't right with her reaction to his news. She acted as if vampires were an everyday occurrence to her. "Aren't you just a little bit scared?"

"More than you can know."

Okay, at least this response was more realistic. "Well, that's what I had to tell you. If what they told us is true, you can't wander around at night without some kind of weapon. The chief suggested a wooden stake."

Julie smiled. "Sorry, fresh out of stakes. I used the last one over a week ago."

"You did?"

"No, silly." She stepped close and ran her hand over his temple, threading her fingers into his hair. "I was just kidding about the stake." Then she smiled for the first time since the night they'd made love. "What is it you wanted to talk about? You didn't look very happy at work this morning? Is it something I did?"

She pressed a finger to his lips then followed it with a kiss. "No. You're perfect. I just…well…" Julie broke contact and left the circle of his arms to pace her living room floor. "I…I am…I have this friend," she finished in a rush.

"I imagine you have lots of friends." He closed the distance between them and reached out to take her back into his arms. "I'm okay with that as long as they're not all guys."

Evading his grasp, she ducked past him and continued her pacing. "Since you've already been briefed that there are vampires in the city, maybe this will make more sense." She glanced at him. When he met her gaze, she looked away again. "If this friend was what your chief said…"

"A vampire?" What was she talking about? Surely she didn't believe all that nonsense about vampires. Although, Roger had to admit he was beginning to lean that direction.

"Let's just say for the sake of argument, I have a friend who is a vampire."

"I'd say you should share some of that wacky weed with me." He smiled to soften his words. "I'm not ready to fall for all that garbage, as convincing as the chief was."

"Okay, say you believe in all that garbage for the sake of my story."

"But I don't."

She threw her hands in the air. "Just pretend, then."

Roger held up his hands. "Okay. I'll pretend I believe in vampires."

"If my friend was a vampire and she seemed normal in every other way but that she was a vampire, would you hate her?"

Roger's brows drew together. He could tell his answer meant a lot to her. "Are you telling me you have a vampire for a friend?"

"Assuming vampires exist, yes."

"If you trusted that friend, then I'd trust your judgment."

"But would you hate that my friend was a vampire?"

More confused than he wanted to admit he told her what he hoped she wanted to hear. "No."

Julie let out a long breath, her stiff shoulders loosening. "Good."

"Good, good." This time when he closed the distance, she didn't back away. Roger pulled her into his arms and kissed her. "I think you're terrific and any friend of yours is a friend of mine."

"One more thing—"

"I'd love anyone you care about. Enough talk. I've been waiting for this since I saw you at the hospital."

Julie gave up. With Roger warm and willing, kissing her on the neck and lower, she could resist no longer. Hell, she'd all but told him she was a vampire and he didn't seem to be repelled by the thought of someone being a vampire. He'd be all right when he learned the truth, wouldn't he?

He lifted her shirt up and over her head and Julie lost her ability to think. Roger's hands were everywhere she wanted them and then some. Her jeans and panties were next to go and she stood naked in front of him.

Julie had never felt as complete with any other man as she did with Roger. He made her whole. Her hands moved to the buttons on his polo shirt, slipping them loose. Then with more eagerness than grace, she yanked it up and over his head, tossing it to the corner where it hung on a floor lamp. Somewhere in the back of her mind she wondered if it would catch fire. Following that thought was the surety the sheets would ignite first.

All her adult life, she'd gone from relationship to relationship despairing of finding a man who shared her interests. Roger cared about people, preferred walking in the rain rather than using an umbrella and liked the same mix of action adventure and science fiction movies. He was a man who enjoyed reading as a form of entertainment and scuba diving. Not that she'd get to do much of that, now that she was a vampire. Her activities would be limited to nocturnal pursuits.

Everything had changed and yet everything was the same.

She was a vampire and couldn't go out in the sun, but she still loved this man who was dropping kisses on her bare shoulder. As his warm, wet tongue flicked at her collarbone, she planted hands on either side of his face and guided him farther south to her left breast. "Ahhh. You're getting warmer."

"You got that right. Too warm." He sucked her breast into his mouth and tugged on it gently. At the same time, he struggled with his belt and the clasp on his jeans. When he almost fell over, his mouth left her breast and he grinned. "I think I need both hands to get out of these."

She liked the way he could joke about the little things and how his smile melted her knees. "Let me help."

With both hands, she grasped the snap and flicked it loose. The zipper slid downward with ease and she had him out of those jeans so fast she surprised even herself. Oh yeah, vampire speed, better than the internet speed on her home computer.

Roger stood in the middle of the room, naked and glorious with brows raised.

A glance downward made her flush with a rush of sensual awareness.

His cock jutted out, hard and full.

A smile curved her lips and she reached out to take his penis into her hands. "Miss me?" Her fingers curled around him, reveling in the dichotomy of velvety soft skin and the steely hardness beneath.

Roger's chest filled with a deep breath and he let it out in a groan. "More than you can imagine." His hands rose to grasp her arms. "You sure you're okay?"

"As good as I can be." Given that I'm a vampire and I don't have the guts to tell you.

"Come here." He pulled her to him, his cock bumping against her belly. "I need to be inside you."

"And I need you there." With one hand, she moved his hand downward guiding his fingers to her clit. Her other hand slid along his length, smoothing over the skin and down to his balls.

"If you're not careful, I won't make it to the whipped cream."

"We can always have dessert later." She lifted one leg, wrapping it around his hip, her cunt pressed against his thigh.

"Don't you want to move into the bedroom?" Two rough fingers pushed up inside her, spreading her open, widening her channel for a much larger insertion.

Her pussy responded with a rush of cream and suddenly every nerve cell in Julie's body ignited, sending heat flaming through her body. "How about here…now." She dropped to the carpet, pulling him down with her.

"What about foreplay?"

"Later." Julie's knees fell open and Roger settled between them, pressing the tip of his cock to her wet pussy.

He paused. "Somehow I pictured this seduction a little differently."

"Are you disappointed?"

He dipped the tip of his cock into her cunt. "No."

"Good." Then she grabbed his firm buttocks and slammed him home. "Fuck me, Roger. Fuck me hard."

He chuckled, his dick sliding in and out in a slow steady rhythm. "My sweet Julie has a dirty mouth."

"Does that bother you when I say that?"

"No, it makes me hot." His pace increased, the friction heating up her insides.

"Then what are you waiting for?" She pulled her knees back to allow him deeper penetration. "I want it hard and fast."

"I can do that." He leaned down over her and kissed her lips. "I never dreamed being with you could feel so good."

With her eyes closed to his gorgeous face, she internalized every stroke, memorizing the feeling of him sliding in and out of her. His thrusts pushed her closer to the edge, the rough fabric of the carpet against her naked buttocks only added to the experience. When he draped her legs over his shoulders and held onto her thighs, she thought she'd come all over him. But she forced her orgasm back, waiting until he was closer.

"Open your eyes, Julie." Roger slowed, dropped her legs from his shoulders and leaned over to kiss her eyelids. "I want to see your eyes when you come."

The gentle touch of his lips coaxed her to open them. With his cock filling her to full and heat burning through her body, her gaze focused on the throbbing pulse in his throat. Oh no. She shouldn't have opened her eyes.

Don't do it, Julie. Don't bite him. You don't need his blood. It felt so good to be fucked by him. The only thing that could maximize the experience was to sink her teeth into his neck and taste the blood coursing through his body.

When his pounding tempo reached a crescendo, Roger dropped down on top of her, gathering her close for one final thrust. His neck was within a hairsbreadth from her lips.

She'd kiss him. Only a kiss.

When her lips pressed against that throbbing pulse, Julie lost all control. She could feel her fangs extending and she couldn't do anything to stop it.

With Roger's final thrust, Julie's teeth sank into his neck.

He stiffened. "What the fuck?" His surprise quickly evaporated as his orgasm shook him from head to toe.

Roger's cock jerked inside Julie with the force of his semen shooting out.

Julie was lost in a heart-stopping explosion of sensations from red-hot blood coursing down her throat to waves of heat spreading from her cunt outward. The combination was overwhelming and completely consuming.

When her desire cooled and her thirst for blood was slaked, Julie released her hold on his neck and she lay back on the bed, wondering if she'd ever felt anything quite like that.

Then she turned to Roger, who'd rolled over next

to her, a smile across his face, his skin a little pale beneath the tan.

Holy crap! Had she taken too much blood? Julie chewed her bottom lip. "You all right?"

"Never felt better." His words were slightly slurred. "What was that you did? I've never had quite so intense an orgasm."

"Me either." He sounded drunk, but alive. Maybe she hadn't overdone it.

One of his hands reached up to touch his neck where she'd bit him. "Did you bite me?"

"Uh…a little." At least she didn't lie. She could have bitten him a lot more.

"That's what I thought." His eyes drifted closed. "I'm very sleepy. Mind if I crash here?"

"I'd love it."

As he drifted off, he whispered, "There's so much I don't know about you."

"No kidding."

"And I want to learn it all." His voice faded, and he was asleep. A deep sleep, almost as if he was dead.

"Roger?" Julie leaned over him and shook his shoulders. "Roger?" Her heart squeezed tight choking off the blood she'd drained from his body. Was he dead? She pressed an ear to his chest.

A faint thrumming sound made her sag over the top of him. Thank God, she hadn't killed him. But what if he died anyway? Luke's victims had died.

Julie leaped from the bed and ran from the room. Before she made it to the door of her apartment, she remembered she was naked and ran back for her robe. When she yanked her front door open, she didn't see William and plowed right into him.

"Whoa." His arms gripped her shoulders and steadied her. "Where's the fire?"

"I think I killed him. You have to help him." Julie grabbed William's arm and hauled him through her living room into the bedroom where Roger lay sprawled across the bed, naked and deathly pale.

"See? He's not usually that pale." Practically shoving William at the man, she cried, "And he won't wake up."

William stood back, staring down at the naked Roger. "Not bad, Julie. I bet he gave you a good ride, huh?" His lips twitched and he crossed his arms over his chest. "Although I think I might have him on the cock."

"What are you saying?" Julie turned to William and clutched his arms. "The man might be dying and you're comparing cocks? Did you hear me? I bit him!"

"I could tell by the flush in your cheeks."

Julie was ready to slap the smile off William's face, she was so frustrated. "Do something!"

"It's okay, Julie. He'll live. As long as he's still breathing." William nodded at Roger. "And he's still breathing. He'll be okay. Calm down."

Julie turned away and paced the length of the bed, gazing down at Roger. "I don't know what came over me. It's as if I couldn't stop myself."

"That ability comes with practice. It's natural for a vampire to bite during an orgasm." He grinned. "Best orgasm you've ever had, wasn't it?"

"Ah, geez." She pressed her hands to her heated cheeks. "Beyond incredible."

"And he didn't mind that you're a vampire?"

Her cheeks burned hotter and she turned away from William. "I sorta didn't tell him."

"You didn't tell him?" William's brows lifted. "I see."

Julie spun to face him. "What do you see? That I'm a coward? That I'm a liar? Well, damn it, I love this man and I don't want to screw things up between us. Not now." She wrung her hands. "We're just starting out."

William raised his hands. "Okay. You don't have to bite me to make a point."

She glanced at the bite marks on Roger's neck. "Will he remember?"

"Not if you don't want him to."

"What do you mean?" Her poor brain already on overload with vampire trivia, Julie forced herself to focus. "And what do I do about the bite? If he wakes up and sees those fang marks, he'll know."

"Another vampire perk. You can lick the wound closed and fade the scar as well as muddy the memory with a little telepathy."

Julie glommed onto that piece of information. "I can do telepathy?"

"With practice."

"Wow. Being a vampire does have some perks." The immortal thing and the strength were a known quantity from the get-go, but telepathy? Cool. She wondered how many more advantages she'd discover and when.

William was shaking his head. "I don't recommend reading minds, though. It can be messy and overwhelming to the neophyte vampire."

"Whatever, as long as I can whitewash this little incident to where Roger doesn't remember that I bit him."

"Is that all you don't want him to remember?" William glanced to where her robe hung open, exposing everything. "What about the sex?"

Wrapping the belt around her middle, she tied it with a jerk. "Oh, I want him to remember that. Can I do that? Wash away one memory without taking all of them?"

"Yes, if you're careful."

She clapped her hands together. "Let's get started. I don't know how long he'll sleep."

A loud rumbling sound woke Roger from a dead sleep. When he realized it was his own stomach, he darted a look over the side of the bed at the clock on the nightstand—6:00 p.m. Huh? The clock was not his, nor was the nightstand and the comforter or even the room.

Roger closed his eyes and reopened them, focusing on the woman walking through the doorway, wearing a silky white robe and her hair up in a towel, turban style. Julie—his angel of mercy and she carried a tray of what smelled like food in her hands.

"Good, you're awake." Julie set the tray on the bed and fluffed the pillows behind his head. "You must have been really tired to sleep so long."

"I have to be to work in an hour." The scent of coffee drew him to the contents of the tray. "Is that for me?"

"Oh, I'm sorry. Yes. Since you slept through breakfast and lunch, I thought you might be hungry." She removed a pan lid from the plate and steam rose from a mouth-watering pile of scrambled eggs, bacon and toast.

His stomach rumbled louder and he reached for the plate. Ravenous, he dug in. Not until he'd eaten several bites did he think to ask. "Aren't you going to eat?"

Julie smoothed the comforter, refusing to meet his gaze. "I ate earlier."

Pain stabbed through his temple and he winced. "Got any pain killers? I feel like I've got the hangover to beat all hangovers."

"Sure. I'll be right back." She raced from the room and was back so fast, Roger barely had time to eat a bite of toast.

"How do you do that?"

"What?"

"Move so fast?" He reached for the tablets and water she handed him and downed them.

"Better?"

"Yeah. Except for the pain in my neck."

"Pain?" She examined his neck with an inordinate amount of curiosity, her eyes widening. "Here, let me rub it for you."

He shifted his head from side to side. "I think I slept on it wrong."

"Oh, right. You slept so long." She moved to sit behind him and massaged the knots in his stiff neck, leaning close to kiss the side that hurt. A warm wet tongue passed over the skin, leaving a trail of tingles.

"Umm, that feels good."

"You like that?" She licked him again and followed by pressing a kiss to the spot. "There, all better." Julie shifted behind him and stood.

The food, pills and massage all combined to make Roger feel much better. He laid the plate on the nightstand. "I don't have to be to work for an hour." Before Julie could get away, Roger snagged her hand and pulled her on top of him.

Her breasts pressed against his chest and her breathing was coming in ragged gasps. "I really think we need to talk."

Roger kissed her lips. "About what?"

"About last night."

He kissed the sensitive area below her earlobe. "Talk away." He rolled her onto her back and spread her robe open.

"About last night…" she began.

"I remember." He worked his way down her body, kissing and nipping the tips of her breasts, counting her ribs as his tongue slid downward. When he reached the soft fur of her mound, he spread her folds wide.

Julie gasped and her back arched. "What do you remember?"

"You were fantastic." His mouth claimed her clit. He flicked and nibbled the nub until her fingers twined in his hair and pulled him even closer. Sliding a hand over her inner thigh, he thrust two fingers into her pussy, swirling in the creamy moisture.

"Do you remember anything else?" Her voice was a breathy whisper he barely heard.

"Yes. I remember." He dragged his wet finger downward and circled her anus. "I remember wanting to do this."

With her asshole moist from her own juices, he probed her, pushing steadily inward until his first knuckle was inside. He pointed the tip of his finger toward her vagina and pressed fingers from his other hand inside her pussy. He could feel the fingers from his other hand through the walls of her vagina. "You're so beautiful," he said, then continued his assault on her clit, stroking her cunt and anus as the same time.

Julie's feet planted in the comforter and her bottom lifted off the bed. "I'm going to come."

"Do it, baby. Come to me." He flicked her clit, laving his tongue over it until she cried out. Then he shoved his fingers all the way inside her asshole and cunt at the same time.

Julie remained taut, her body jerking with her release. When her ass fell back to the bed, Roger climbed up her body and sank his cock deep inside her wet cunt. He rocked against her, the walls of her pussy clutching at his dick, pulling him deeper. She was so tight, so delicious. "I could do this forever," he said against her neck and pumped in and out of her with a fierce longing to do just that. In a short amount of time, this woman had crawled into his heart—a heart he thought unable to love again after his ex-wife's betrayal. Julie was his angel, a woman incapable of deception, unable to hurt others with lies. His body surged and shot him to the edge. Just as he toppled over and released inside her, he cried out. "I love you, Julie."

Her body went rigid and she lay stiff and unmoving beneath him. "You can't love me, Roger. You don't know me."

Roger had never been packed off and pushed out of a house so fast. What had he said? "I just don't get it. I told her I loved her."

Too confused and not feeling on top of his form, Roger had insisted Chase do the driving for their shift. Darkness had already filled the sky and the street lights glowed an ominously eerie yellow.

Chase scratched his jaw. "Too soon, you think?"

"I guess. I thought all women wanted the man to say those three words."

"You keep telling me Julie isn't like other women."

"I'm beginning to believe it more and more." The more he thought about last night, the more he realized Julie wasn't acting quite like herself. "She more or less told me her friend is a vampire."

Chase shot a quick glance his way. "She's buying

all that crap? I thought the chief was feeding us a line of bull."

"Me too. But it's got me worried."

"How so?"

"That man who attacked us outside the restaurant the other night. Julie knew his name."

"Did she say how?"

"No. I know, I should have asked." Roger was still kicking himself for not delving into that question more thoroughly. "Problem is, every time I'm around her…"

"You can't think past your dick," Chase finished.

"Yeah. Pretty much." He shook his head. "Do you think there's any truth to Kim being a vampire?"

"She looks she could be. What with all that black makeup and her black hair, she looks like the dead."

"Maybe we should keep an eye on her."

They turned a corner and the lights from the hospital lit the night.

"Hey, isn't that Kim, now?"

She'd parked her car in a ground lot and walked toward the hospital, hiking her purse up onto her shoulder.

Roger grabbed the door handle. "Let me out here."

"What are you going to do?" Chase slowed the cruiser.

"Talk to her."

"You think she'll admit it if she's a vampire?"

He smacked the dash with the palm of his hand. "I

don't know. Stop, will you. She's almost to the hospital. I want to catch her before she goes in."

Kim Erickson headed toward the back entrance. She had to pass the large dumpsters and an alley entrance before she entered the back door.

When Chase pulled against the curb, Roger jumped out and hurried after her. If she was a vampire, he'd know soon enough. "Kim!"

The woman jumped and spun to face Roger, a can of mace in her hand. "Stop, or I'll shoot."

Roger laughed, holding up his hands. "It's just me."

"Roger?" As she walked back toward him, her shoulders relaxed. "What are you doing here? Julie doesn't come on for another hour."

"I wanted to talk to you."

Her forehead crinkled into a frown. "About what?"

"Something Julie told me last night."

"She told you?" Kim's eyes widened. "Oh, thank goodness. I hate keeping secrets. You're okay with it?"

"Yes," Roger answered slowly, wondering if they were talking about the same thing.

"I didn't know if you'd believe the vampire part. You must be pretty open-minded for a cop."

Okay so they were talking about the same thing. "Yeah. I guess I am. So how long has she known?"

"Oh it only happened four nights ago. She's still trying to get used to the idea."

"It is hard to believe."

"I know. It still amazes me—vampires in Houston."

"So how can you tell if someone's a vampire?"

"Besides the not moving around during the daytime, it's pretty tough."

"What about the fangs? Aren't they pretty obvious?"

"Vampires can hide their fangs. Did you know that?"

"No, I didn't know that."

"Yeah. Vampires can move very fast and have the strength of three men." She squinted at him. "You sure that doesn't bother you?"

"As long as you're not throwing me around, why should it?"

"Me?" She jerked her thumb at her chest. "But I'm n—"

A roar from the alley jerked Roger's attention from Kim. He turned in time to see Luke, the blond vampire, hurtling toward him. With no time to react, Roger hunkered into a football blocking stance and braced himself for impact.

When Luke hit him, Roger was thrown back, landing hard on his tailbone. He tucked and rolled, but not before Luke got his hands on him.

The vampire grabbed Roger's uniform shirt and lifted him high into the air. "Leave my woman alone!"

Roger knew he was talking about Julie. "She's not your woman."

"Yes, she is. I turned her, she's mine." Then he threw Roger as easily as a farmer tosses a bale of hay. Roger arced through the air and slammed against the metal dumpster, the wind knocked from his lungs.

While Roger struggled to fill his lungs, Chase leaped from the squad car and fired on the crazed vampire.

Other than jerking his body a little, the bullets did nothing to stop the man. Luke charged toward Chase and plowed into him like a steamroller. The cop hit the car and slid down the door in an unconscious heap.

Gathering his strength, Roger clambered to his feet and gulped in air.

Luke laughed and grabbed for Kim, sinking his teeth into her neck.

The woman struggled for only a moment, then went limp in the vampire's arms.

Anger fueled Roger's movements, making him forget the bumps and bruises he'd accumulated. He was responsible for the safety and wellbeing of this city's inhabitants. He couldn't let Luke kill Kim. The vampire had to die, but how? His gaze shot around the area and he spied a wooden pallet lying next to the dumpster. With strength born of desperation, he lifted the pallet and slammed it against the dumpster until a slat broke loose. He cracked the slat over the corner of the dumpster. The wood splintered and Roger turned to Luke, jagged stake in hand.

Kim lay across Luke's arm, her head dropped

back, neck exposed to his bite and he was sucking the life out of her.

"Put her down!" Roger charged the stake held out in front of him.

Luke dropped Kim to the ground and roared like a savage animal.

Roger aimed for the heart as instructed.

Luke twisted to the side. The stake caught him on the arm and broke in two pieces. The vampire's hand swept out, catching Roger in the chest knocking him twenty feet backward.

The last thing Roger remembered was Luke lifting Kim and continuing his meal. Then all went black.

Julie didn't have to report to work until midnight, but she wanted to get there right before Kim went on duty. She needed to talk to someone about what she'd done and hadn't done. Her full stomach reveled in the blood she'd siphoned from Roger at the same time it churned. How could she lose herself so much she'd bite the one man she loved? Was the lie she lived eating her from the inside out? Had she gone rotten to the core?

Perhaps the temptations of being a vampire were much harder to control than she'd originally thought. Which would explain why some vampires went bad, like Luke Hester. Speaking of which, something had to be done to stop him before he hurt anyone else.

William had gone out on a mission to find Luke and bring him down.

In the meantime, Julie needed a friend, and Kim was the only one who knew what challenges she faced.

Because her car was still on the fritz, Julie had to walk to the hospital. Even with her vampire strengths and abilities, the night still creeped her out. Not good. As a recently turned creature of the night, she would have to get used to moving about in the dark. No more long soaks in the sun for her. Not that she ever did. Her strawberry blonde hair condemned her to a life out of the sun from the day she was born. She'd never been a morning person, preferring the night shift for work and the day for sleeping. She could have it worse, she supposed.

As she neared the hospital, a scream ripped through the air. Her feet kicked into gear and she ran toward the sound. "Put her down!" Damn, that was Roger's voice.

Julie cut through the alley behind the hospital and ran into Luke Hester with a fang-lock on Kim's throat.

Kim sagged against him, her eyes closed and her face whiter than her Goth makeup.

Rage roared through Julie and she grabbed Luke by the collar, yanking him off Kim. With all her strength, she flung him at the brick wall of the hospital.

That didn't slow him down long. Luke picked himself off the ground and shouted, "She's mine and so are you."

"Shut up or I'll dust your ass." Julie bent over Kim to check for a pulse, her own pulse pounding so hard against her ears she couldn't hear. Had he drained her friend? Would she die?

Kim's skin was cool to the touch and she didn't respond when Julie shook her.

"Kim?" Julie couldn't feel a pulse in her friend's throat. Fuck! The bastard killed her.

Before she could rise to her feet, a hand clamped in Julie's hair and she was yanked off her feet and dragged on her ass backward toward the alley.

"You are my woman." Luke had her in a caveman grip and he was hauling her off to she didn't know where and frankly didn't want to know.

She scrambled to get her feet under her, but at the pace he was pulling her, she couldn't. Her scalp burned where her hair held the weight of her body. Julie rolled to the side, twisting Luke's arm.

Before they reached the end of the alley, a man jumped across the entrance. "In the name of the Father, the Son and the Holy Ghost, die!" Bob Marley blocked Luke's way, a crossbow braced against his shoulder.

Luke threw back his head and laughed.

Although Luke still had a grip on her hair, he'd stopped and Julie could get her feet underneath her.

An arrow whizzed through the air and struck Luke in the shoulder, missing his heart by a good four inches.

Luke screamed and let go of Julie's hair. He jerked

the arrow from his shoulder and ran toward Bob Marley before the vampire hunter could reload.

Julie followed, sure Bob was a goner. Luke looked mad enough to kill the man who wanted to kill him, and her, for that matter. Yet, Julie couldn't let Luke kill Bob, the man was on a mission from God in his mind, and Luke was one badass vampire worthy of Bob's wooden arrow.

The nurse in her forced her to follow. She had to stop Luke's killing rampage.

The vampire backhanded the crossbow from Bob's hand and lifted him by the collar with a single hand. When Bob was four feet from the ground and his face was turning a deep shade of purple, the wooden arrow he still held, slipped from his hand and fell to the pavement.

If she didn't do something quickly, Luke would kill Marley. Julie dove for the weapon as Luke's arms flexed to launch the man through the air. Without thinking, she snatched the arrow from the ground, rolled to her feet and jammed it into Luke's chest, straight through the heart.

Luke's eyes widened and he let go of Bob to clutch at the arrow buried in his heart.

Bob Marley crumpled to the ground, gasping.

"You were mine," Luke said, his voice a pathetic whine.

"You're wrong there." Julie stood with her feet spread wide, her hands perched on her hips. "I belong to no one."

Before he could say more, Luke imploded in a cloud of putrid dust, the stench similar to wet campfire ash.

Brushing the dust from her eyes, Julie saw a movement.

The vampire hunter scuttled across the pavement, reaching for his crossbow and quiver of arrows.

Julie rolled her eyes. "Don't you ever give up?"

"Not until every last vampire is dead. It's my duty." He stood, his hands shaking as he fit an arrow into the crossbow.

"I got him, you check on the others," a voice said over her shoulder.

Julie jumped and stared at William standing next to her. "Damn! How do you do that?"

He grinned. "Practice. Now go."

As Julie turned, William grabbed the crossbow and slammed it against a nearby brick wall. The weapon shattered into a million pieces.

Not to be deterred, Bob held a wood arrow in front of him. "I have to kill vampires. They're abominations."

"That vampire just saved your sorry ass." William jerked his head toward Julie. "Get it through your thick skull, not all vampires are bad."

Bob's hand wavered. "Yes, they are."

Julie glanced over her shoulder.

William reached out and took the arrows from his hands, snapping them in two. Then he tossed the arrows as far as he could throw. "Leave us alone so that we can check on our friends. They aren't vampires and they need medical attention."

Julie didn't wait for Bob's response, she turned her back on the two men and loped back the way she'd come.

"I'll let you get away this time, but not next time," Bob called out.

"Whatever." Julie emerged from the alley and scanned the scene. It looked like a war zone. Kim, Roger and his partner were all lying on the ground. Since she was practically sure Kim wasn't going to make it, she hurried to Roger and Chase. They each had a steady pulse and were breathing.

Chase stirred and struggled to sit up. "What the hell happened?"

"Vampire attack. Stay down until I get help." Her heart aching for her friend, Julie returned to Roger. She felt along his arms and legs for broken bones.

"What are we going to do with her?" William dropped to his knees next to Kim, a frown pressing his brows together.

Julie's chest tightened. "She's dead, isn't she?"

"Almost."

"Almost?" Julie glanced at Roger. His pulse was steady and his body warm. She'd help him in a minute. Kim's needs were more pressing. "Can we save her if we get her into the hospital?"

"No. It's too late for that. For all intents and purposes, she'll die. The question is, are you willing to let her die or grant her immortality?"

"I can do that?"

"She's your friend. You know her better than I do." William lifted Kim's head into his lap and smoothed the black hair back from her white forehead. "Do you think she'd want the option to become one of us?"

The bottom fell out of Julie's stomach. It was one thing to be turned when it wasn't your option. Given the choice, would Kim prefer to die or would she want to become a vampire and live forever? Julie snorted. "Easy. She's fascinated by vampires. I think she'd want to live." Kim lay so quietly in William's arms, so out of character for the talkative Goth freak. "What do we do?"

"I'll need a knife."

Julie raced to Rogers's side and rummaged in his pocket. He always carried a small pocket knife. She knew that from when he'd emptied his pockets onto her nightstand. When she found it, she pressed a kiss to his forehead. "I'll get you help as soon as we take care of Kim." Without wasting time, she hurried back to William. "I want to do this."

William's brows rose. "Are you sure?"

"Yes."

"Then bite her. After the third bite, give her back your blood."

Julie shivered. She'd bitten Roger in the heat of passion. Biting a dying woman seemed so cold.

"Either do it or don't," William bit out, his face

strained as he stared down at Kim. "But decide quickly or she'll die anyway."

Julie nodded. If Kim was going to be mad, it might as well be at her. She leaned over Kim, positioning her mouth farther down from where Luke had sunk his fangs into her throat. Breathing deeply, she concentrated on her bloodlust and extending her fangs. Then she bit into Kim and sucked her blood, falling into the passion of feeding off a living human being. If not for William's hand on her shoulder, she'd have been lost. She pulled her fangs free and sat back, wiping the blood from her lips. The horror of what she'd just done made her stomach rise.

"Don't stop now. One more time. She has to be bitten three times." William pushed her toward Kim's throat for the last bite.

This time, she fought the urge to forget where she was and what she as doing. Kim needed her to stay focused. When she surfaced the second time, William handed her the knife.

He closed his fingers around hers and held her hand for a brief moment. "Vampires heal quickly, but they feel pain just the same."

"I can do this," Julie said, as much to convince herself as to convince William. She flipped the blade open, took a deep breath and sliced across her wrist.

Pain seared through her and she bit down hard on her lip to keep from crying out.

"Hurry." William said. "Her life force is slipping

away. The sooner she drinks the vampire's blood, the better chance we have of turning her."

Blood oozed from the wound and dripped onto the ground. Julie knelt beside her friend and pressed the bloody wrist to Kim's lips. "Please, Kim. Live."

CHAPTER 10

When Roger opened his eyes, he stared up at the street lamp over his head and tried to remember where he was and what the hell happened. The image of the big, blond vampire biting into Kim's throat surfaced as his last conscious thought and he jerked to a sitting position.

A few yards away, Julie and her neighbor, William, kneeled next to Kim's limp body and Julie had her wrist pressed to Kim's mouth.

"What are you doing?" Roger asked.

Julie's gaze darted to his, her eyes wide and… guilty? Then a jerky smile lifted the corners of her lips. "Oh Roger, you're awake. Please, stay where you are until I can get the ER staff out here to assist you."

Why didn't she just answer him? He climbed to his feet, staggering a few steps beneath the weight of a pounding headache and a twisted ankle. "I don't want assistance. I want to know what the hell you're doing. Is that blood?"

Red liquid dripped down the side of Kim's mouth.

Julie glanced down at her friend, her face soft and worried. "We're trying to save Kim."

"She's bleeding. Shouldn't she be the one in the ER room?"

"It's too late for that." Julie's mouth twisted. "Besides, it's not her blood. It's mine."

He crossed the pavement toward them. "What do you mean?"

"She's already dead," Julie said in a whisper, her gaze soft as she stared down at her friend. "All we can hope to do is turn her."

What was she saying? Roger pushed across his scalp. Hell, even his hair hurt. "Turn her to what?"

Julie stared up at him. "A vampire."

He stopped in mid-stride. Had he heard her right? "But isn't she already a vampire?"

As Julie shook her head, he traced back through his conversation with her earlier. "But you said your friend…" He stopped and thought again. "Kim's not the vampire?"

Julie shook her head again.

Roger looked across at William. "Him?"

"Well, yes. William is a vampire." As Julie rose to her feet, tears trembled on the edges of her eyelids. "But he's not the only one I was talking about."

"You mean you have more friends who are vampires?"

She shook her head. "No. I was really talking about me."

"You?" Roger sucked in a deep breath as her words sank in. "You're a vampire?"

"Yes." Julie's chin lifted and she met his gaze. "I'm a vampire."

"Wait. Let me get this straight." Roger tipped his head to the side, his brain slogging through that last little bit she'd said. "You're a what?"

"Vampire."

He inhaled and let it out before asking, "Have you always been?"

"No." She pressed a hand to the wrist that had been bleeding, but the blood was already drying, the wound closing.

"How long have you been a…a…?" He couldn't say it, much less believe what she said. Not his sweet Julie.

"A vampire." She sighed. "I've been a vampire since the night before our first date."

"All this time we've been together, you knew?"

She nodded, her shoulders sagging. "I didn't know how to tell you."

He clamped a hand to his neck. "Did you…"

"Bite you?" Her gaze dropped to her feet. "Once."

That's why his neck had hurt so much. "Last night?"

"Yes."

"Look, Decker, she didn't tell you, because she didn't want to lose you. If you can't handle that she's a vampire, that's your problem." William stood, lifting Kim in his arms. She still lay limp and lifeless, but color was beginning to return to her cheeks. "I need to get her to the apartment before morning."

Julie nodded to William "Go ahead. I'll see you before dawn."

After William left. Julie faced Roger, her shoulders pushing back. "Are you going to tell anyone?"

"Hey, Decker," Parker's voice called out behind him.

Roger turned toward his friend. "I'm here. You all right?"

"Other than a Texas-sized headache, I think I'll live." Parker climbed to his feet and staggered over to Roger. "What happened to Mr. Nasty?"

"He's gone," Julie answered, her gaze on Roger. "For good."

Roger nodded.

Parker scrubbed a hand over his face. "Guess what the chief said was true. We got us some vampires kickin' ass in the city."

"Yeah." Roger felt as though he'd been kicked in the gut. Vampires in the city, having his ass pounded by one, then finding out his girlfriend was one of the bad guys and she'd bit him all in one day was more than he could handle. "Come on Parker, let's get back to the station and report what happened." He couldn't look at Julie. Wouldn't.

Her hand shot out and caught his arm. "Are you going to report everything?"

For a long moment, he stared at her hand. He couldn't believe she was a vampire. She looked just like she'd always looked. The part that bothered him most was that she didn't trust him enough to tell him. When he gazed into her eyes, his jaw tightened. "I don't know what I'm going to do."

William took Kim back to his apartment to keep an eye on her through the night and Julie reported to work on time. If her uniform was a little dirty and her hair a mess, she couldn't help it. Frankly, she didn't care. Roger had walked away from her without kissing her goodbye.

By the look on his face when he'd left, he might never kiss her again.

When she got a free moment, Julie called William. Kim hadn't woken yet, but he felt certain they'd caught her in time.

"You comin' down with what Kim has?" Nurse Lindeman stepped up next to her at the nurses station, a chart open in her hands.

Julie almost laughed at how close the head nurse was to the truth. "Definitely."

Lindeman completed her notes on the clipboard and handed it to the nurse behind the counter, before she turned to face Julie. "It's kinda of slow around here, why don't you go home? We can handle the rest of the shift."

She wasn't sure she wanted to go home, but her mind wasn't on the care of her patients. All she could think about was Roger and whether or not he'd forgive her and accept her for what she was. Yes, she needed a long walk to clear her mind. "If you're sure you don't mind."

Lindeman gave her one of her rare smiles and pushed her toward the door. "Go on."

Before the head nurse could change her mind, Julie left the ER and walked as fast as she could, putting as much distance between her and the hospital as she could. The farther she went the more she realized she couldn't walk away from her problems. If Roger chose never to see her again, she'd have to live with that. She couldn't undo what Luke had done, and she couldn't stop being a vampire to make Roger want to see her again.

When she finally looked up, she was standing in front of the old apartment house. Sitting on the steps in front was Roger.

Her heart skidded to a halt and her breath lodged in her throat. Roger had come back.

As soon as he saw her, he stood and glanced toward the sky. "Shouldn't you be getting inside? It'll be dawn soon."

Julie nodded and pulled her key from her purse. She had to walk past him to get to the door. The scent of his cologne and the smell of leather combined to make every one of her nerves stand up and shout hallelujah. Roger was back.

Why?

Moving past him, she entered the house and climbed the stairs to her apartment. At her door, she paused with the key poised to slide into the door-knob. "Why are you here?"

"We need to talk." His jaw was as tight as it had been when he'd left her earlier and the scowl on his forehead didn't bode well.

Julie nodded and shoved the key into the lock. A flash of anger surged through her. For the past two hours, she'd been wandering the streets wondering whether or not she'd ever see Roger and here he was. Happiness was the appropriate reaction, and she might have been happy if not for the fierce look and feel to the cop following her into her apartment.

As soon as Roger closed the door behind him, he turned to grab Julie's arms. "Why?"

That seemed to be the question *du jour.*

She knocked his hands away and fisted her hands on her hips. "Why what?"

"Why did you lie to me? Why couldn't you just tell me the truth?"

"I tried. But I couldn't."

Roger shook his head, his lips twisting. "I thought you were the one. The only woman I could trust… and then this." He strode across the room and back. "Why?"

"You think I wanted to be a vampire? My life was on track. Great job, a man interested in me and me in him. Then bam!" She threw her arms in the air. "One day I'm human, the next I'm a vampire. I could barely accept it myself. How was I supposed to tell you?"

"The truth would have been a good start."

"Well, I didn't. Okay? So I'm flawed, I'm not perfect."

"I don't expect you to be perfect. I just expect you to tell me the important stuff."

"Just because I'm a vampire, doesn't change who I am inside. I still have feelings, I can still love." Her anger evaporated and she sagged onto the arm of the couch. What was the use? He couldn't love her. She was a monster.

Roger strode to her and gripped her arms, lifting her to her feet. "I was so in love with you. I wanted us to be together forever." His words came out hard and fast, as if he forced them out. "We were good together."

She stared into his eyes. "So what's changed?"

"Everything."

Julie couldn't take any more of this, not from the man she'd thought she loved. Tears welled in her eyes and one slid down her cheek. "If that's the way you feel, there's the door. Why don't you use it? Go!" If he walked out, she didn't know what she'd do. He was the only man she cared about. The only one she could see herself spending her life with. Now that she could be stuck with eternity, he was still the one. "You heard me, go."

His grip tightened until his fingers dug into her arms. "I can't." Then he was kissing her, his mouth slanting hard over hers, his tongue pushing past her teeth to tangle with hers, thrusting hard.

In the back of her mind, she knew she should

push him away and toss him out of her apartment. They hadn't resolved anything between them. The kiss was only clouding the issues and putting off decisions that had to be made.

As the kiss deepened, Julie gave herself up to the rise of desire welling inside. This was where she wanted to be. Surely they could work things out.

Roger's fingers loosened on her arms and his hands blazed a path down to her hips. With a not so gentle jerk, he yanked her against him until his engorged cock pressed into her belly. "You do this to me."

Her pelvis rocked automatically, rubbing against the hard ridge of his zipper. She wanted him inside her, fucking her.

"What have you done to me?" he said. "I can't trust you, and I can't get enough of you."

The growl in his voice sent waves of intense longing burning through her. Cream leaked between her legs, wetting the path to her core. No longer content to wait, she squeezed her hands between them and wriggled his trouser button loose. The zipper streaked downward until his trousers fell open. That rigid hunk of male anatomy pushed against snowy white briefs, creating a tempting tent she couldn't resist.

His hands dipped beneath her scrubs shirt and rose up her rib cage to her lacy bra. Her nipples puckered into tight beads of anticipation. Her shirt flew up over her head, and into the far corner, her pants following. When she stood in nothing but her bra and panties, her entire body shook and it was all she could do to restrain herself from using her strength to toss this man into her bed and fuck him like there was no tomorrow.

Tomorrow.

Her resolve to settle things resurfaced in a momentary flash of conscience.

Then Roger slid her bra straps over her shoulders and downward.

Her skin quivered against the rough texture of his fingertips and all thought fled. The sooner she was completely naked, the sooner she could have him inside her filling the void of longing making her pussy moist.

He jerked the clasp loose and flung her bra to the wall, quickly followed by her panties. Then he bent to rasp his tongue across first one then the other nipple, pulling the second one into his mouth and sucking hard.

The answering tug deep inside made her hands rise to his hair and pull him closer. "Please."

While his lips teased her breast, his fingers dove south, skimming across her abdomen to the furry mound between her thighs.

Of their own accord, her legs parted, giving him greater access to her clit, knotted with highly sensitive nerves.

His hands circled behind her and clasped her buttocks, kneading the fleshy mounds and then he scooped behind each thigh and wrapped her legs around his waist.

Her pussy rubbed along the length of his cock and she moaned.

Without a word, Roger strode into the bedroom and laid her out on the bed, spreading her legs wide. Within a few brief movements, he was out of his clothing and climbing onto the mattress. His mouth lowered and he nipped at her inner thighs, tracing a path to the apex and her creamy cunt.

Julie raised her knees and let them fall to the side, opening herself wider to his assault. When his tongue touched against her pussy, her buttocks squeezed tight, raising her off the mattress and into his mouth.

His fingers replaced his tongue, pushing into her pussy with three digits. His mouth moved upward to find and tease her clitoris, strumming the tightly wound nerves in the swollen nub.

Cum-coated fingers slid up her cleft and parted her folds, exposing her to the cool air, the shock of cold meets hot exciting her even more.

Ripples of sensation bubbled within and built like carbonation in a sealed soda bottle. All it would take was a little more and…

Roger dragged a finger from her pussy to the tight lips of her anus.

Yeah. That would make her soda bottle explode for sure. Julie rose up, wanting the connection, praying he'd finger-fuck her asshole. "Do it," she whispered. "Do it."

Then his finger pressed into the hole, past one knuckle to the next. His mouth traveled back to her pussy and his tongue darted in, lapping at her channel.

Julie reached between her legs and stroked her clit, her heels digging into the mattress as her insides surged to the rhythm of Roger's strokes.

Her muscles tensed as she neared the edge and then she blew her cap, exploding into a jillion splinters of light. Her body rode hard against Roger's tongue and finger, shuddering with the sheer intensity of her orgasm.

When she finally fell back to earth, her legs fell to the side, limp and shaking. When Julie thought she couldn't take any more, Roger rose to his knees between her legs and shoved a pillow beneath her ass. Then he drove his cock into her moisture-slick channel. He held her hips, thrusting in and out, his balls slapping against her anus, sexy sucking sounds accompanying his movements.

Pushing upward, she met him thrust for thrust, until he slammed into her one last time. His head tipped backward and he held her tightly against him, his cock pulsing within her channel.

He felt good inside her, his girth stretching the walls of her pussy taut. Julie wished they could always find pleasure in each other. Always be together.

Roger fell to the bed beside her and pulled her into the crook of his arms.

Julie lay there, afraid to say anything to disturb the tenuous truce. As the sun rose over the city, she fell into a troubled sleep.

~

ROGER LEFT Julie's place around noon and drove back to his apartment. He couldn't wait around for her to wake and didn't want to explain his actions, not when he didn't understand them himself.

He'd just fucked a vampire. What troubled him was that he wanted to do it again and again. Not because she was a vampire, but because she was Julie. The woman he'd fallen in love with.

If only she hadn't lied to him. If only she'd been up-front about being turned right when it had happened instead of hiding it from him. She was no better than his ex-wife.

Roger knew he wasn't being fair. Julie had a heart of gold. She gave of herself in everything she did. Her patients loved her, she'd even given Bob Marley the benefit of a doubt and let him live when she could have justifiably killed him for trying to kill her.

Was his problem that he didn't want to love Julie? Was he looking for any excuse to avoid committing to her?

Okay, so she was a vampire. That was a pretty big reason not to commit to the woman.

Except she was still the same Julie deep down. So, she'd kept a secret from him. Would he have believed her from the start? Hell, he barely believed it now. If it hadn't been for the vampire named Luke slamming him around, he might still doubt her word.

Standing beneath the showerhead, Roger let the warm spray beat into his skin, no closer to a decision on what to do about Julie than when he'd shown up at her apartment early that morning. He knew he couldn't wash her out of his system as easily as he could wash the soap from his hair and he wasn't sure he wanted to. Without a doubt, he had to see her again.

CHAPTER 11

Julie went through the motions of getting ready for work that evening, unable to generate any enthusiasm for her shift in the ER. Usually, she looked forward to talking with her coworkers and caring for patients. Not tonight.

Roger was gone when she'd awoken. Nothing had changed. She still didn't have a clue where they stood, but she felt like he was slipping away. Why should he stay with her? She was a freak, a monster, a frickin' vampire. Roger deserved a woman who could bear him children, grow old with him and not bite him when they're making love.

She couldn't promise she'd be able to control her bloodlust in the midst of passion. Last night she was still satisfied with her previous feeding on Roger and Kim, otherwise, she might have done it again.

When she walked out of her apartment, she realized it was raining and she didn't care. Sooner or later, she'd have to deal with getting her car fixed. That would be a task in itself. A neophyte to vampire living, she hadn't learned the ins and outs of moving about in daylight. In order to get her car fixed, she'd have to soon.

As she slogged through the puddles, the rain beat down against her broken umbrella matching her mood. So lost in her own self-pity, Julie didn't realize she was being followed until a man grabbed her from behind, making her drop her umbrella into the gutter.

Without looking back, Julie knew it was Bob Marley. She could tell by the way he smelled. There was another prominent scent she recognized, but couldn't quite put a name to. Another perk William hadn't bothered to tell her about—heightened olfactory senses. "Hello, Bob."

"I let you go last night because you saved my life," he said, his coffee breath wafting over her shoulder. "I can't let you go now."

She could take him, but first she had to try reasoning with the zealot. "Give it up Bob. You can't go around killing all the vampires. We're not all bad."

"Vampires are abomin—"

"I know, I know. You think we're abominations. Well, let me tell you, despite the fact I'm a vampire, I'm a damned good nurse and there are people depending on me to help them through the night.

Now are you going to let me go so I can get to work, or do I have to shake you loose?"

"Vampires must be destroyed. I can't let you go." Though his voice wavered, his grip didn't.

"The hell you can't." Julie shook her head, regret waning and irritation taking hold. As she dropped into a ready stance, a cotton handkerchief covered her nose and mouth and she fought to breathe which answered another question she hadn't thought to ask. Did vampires have to breathe? She sure the hell felt like she needed to.

The acrid scent of chloroform filled her nostrils and dulled her senses, the fuzzy edges of her vision fading into pitch black. Fuck, she'd let herself get caught by the vampire slayer.

~

"YOU DECIDE what you're going to do about your vampire girlfriend?" Parker had gone almost the entire shift without mentioning Julie until they were headed back to the station at the end of their shift.

The sun wouldn't rise for another hour and Roger planned to be in bed before it did. Thinking about Julie was sure to keep him wide-awake for hours, now. "What's it to you?"

"Just curious. I wouldn't mind dating a babe who'll still look young when I'm old, bald and wrinkled."

"Forget it." He glared across the front seat at Parker and then refocused on his driving.

"I thought for sure you'd dump her."

Roger parked the sedan in the station parking lot, turned off the engine and then sat staring at the dash. "I haven't decided."

"Sounds like you're stuck on her." Parker shook his head. "Damn. I was going to make my move. Think she'd kick my ass like she did that big bad vampire?"

"Probably. If she didn't I would."

"So you are staking your claim?"

"I'd rather you didn't use that term."

"Stake?" Parker chuckled. "Uh, sorry."

Roger climbed out of the car, hoping his partner would drop the subject. If he didn't, he'd be forced to make him drop it.

As Parker opened his mouth to say something else, Roger's personal cell phone vibrated on his utility belt. He fumbled to answer, scanning the number in the hope it was Julie. He almost didn't answer when he didn't recognize the number, but instinct told him he'd better. At 4:30 a.m., whoever it was might be in trouble.

"Decker."

"Roger? This is Kim."

"Kim?" The woman who'd almost died because he couldn't save her from a vampire? Hell she was a vampire now, wasn't she? "How are you?"

"Different, that's for sure. But okay." She paused and then asked, "Have you seen Julie?"

"Not since yesterday around noon." She'd been sound asleep, her blonde hair splayed across the white pillowcase, her face angelic, her lips swollen and sexy.

"Damn. She didn't show for work last night. I had a message on my answering machine when I got home a little while ago. Nurse Lindeman wanted to know if I'd seen her. It's not like her to ditch work."

Something akin to a lead wrecking ball crashed at the pit of Roger's gut. As sure as he was crazy about her, he knew Julie was in trouble.

"William and I walked the route she would have taken to work and found her umbrella in the gutter. You have to help. Can you put out an all-points bulletin or something?"

Roger's brain kicked into high gear. Julie was missing. "There are only two people I know who were after her—that Luke guy and Marley."

"Luke's dust. Which leaves Marley. I looked him up in the phone book but couldn't find a phone number or address. Can you do some police mojo and locate him? I wouldn't bother you but it's getting close to dawn and Julie needs to be safely indoors before the sun comes up."

"I'll do what I can." He'd tear the fucking city apart to find her.

"Thanks. Call me when you know anything."

"Will do." Roger flipped his phone shut and jumped out of the car.

Parker followed, running to keep up with him. "What happened?"

He swallowed hard against the lump in his throat before he could answer. "Julie's missing."

"Damn." Parker hit the swinging glass doors into the station before Roger and held it for him to pass through. "The big blond vampire?"

"No. Kim says he's dust."

"Marley."

"That's my bet." He hoped he wasn't too late. Marley had been hell-bent on killing every vampire in the city. Would he hesitate with Julie? Hadn't she saved his life? Didn't he owe her? Roger sank into his desk chair and powered up his computer,

tapping his fingers as the screen booted. In less than a minute he had Marley's address and phone number printing on a clean sheet of paper. As soon the printer released the sheet, Roger was on his feet and headed for the door.

Parker followed on Roger's heels. "You'll need backup."

"Thanks. We're off shift, we'll have to take my truck." Roger crossed the parking lot to his SUV.

"Wait, I have a strobe. Let's take mine." Parker led the way to his brand-new black Mustang. He climbed in the driver's seat and reached behind into the back for a bubble light with a powerful magnet. Once he popped it on top of the vehicle, he squealed out of the parking lot and hit sixty in less than twenty seconds.

Except for the strobe on top, Roger wished he was driving his own truck. The effort of keeping the vehicle on the road at high speeds would have taken his mind off what they might find at Marley's apartment.

The dark night sky gave way to the battleship gray of predawn, and with it, Roger's heart hung heavy in his chest. One more block, just one more block. They would make it. He hoped like hell Marley had taken her to his place. If he hadn't, they'd be too late to find her anywhere else.

When they pulled up beside an older apartment building located in the seedier part of the city, Roger didn't wait for the car to stop, he leaped out and ran for the building. According to the address, Marley lived on the top floor of the four-story building. Racing through the entrance, Roger didn't expect to see an elevator, he headed for the stairs and climbed them two at a time.

By the time he reached the fourth floor, his heart raced and he was gulping in air.

He stopped and held his breath to listen. Was that a sound on the roof?

Parker's feet pounded up the stairs behind him. When he reached the top, he collapsed against the wall beside Roger. "Wh...which...room?" he asked between breaths.

"The end of the hall, but I think there's someone on the roof."

"Marley?"

"Maybe."

"I'll go for the apartment, you take the roof." Parker pushed away from the wall and pulled his Glock.

Having located the stairway to the roof, Roger was halfway up when he heard Parker kick in the door to Marley's apartment. Torn between the roof and the apartment, Roger charged upward. His gut told him the roof, but what if he was wrong? He didn't have time to second-guess. The door to the roof was locked. Roger put his shoulder to it and slammed against it. Wood splintered but the lock held. He hit it again and the door broke open.

As he stepped out onto the roof, the cold barrel of a pistol pressed against his temple.

"Make a move for you gun and I'll shoot."

That's when Roger spotted Julie lying on the flat tarred roof, her hands tied to a clothesline pole.

"That's right. I decided not to kill her. I'd let nature do it for me."

"The sun? You're going to let her fry in the sun?" Roger's stomach roiled at the vivid image playing out in his mind. He could almost smell the scent of seared flesh. Julie's flesh.

His hand jerked toward his pistol.

"I wouldn't if I were you. A bullet might not kill her, but it sure as hell would kill a human."

"Bastard," Roger said through gritted teeth.

"No. That's where you got it wrong. I'm just like you."

"You're nothing like me."

"I'm here to protect people. Isn't that what a cop does?"

"This is wrong. She can't help it she's a vampire. She's got just as much right to live as you do."

"They're parasites. How can it be wrong to rid the world of parasites? These creatures live off the blood of others. It's morally and biblically wrong. Don't you see? They have to die."

"All I see is a man murdering a woman."

"Come now, she didn't tell you she was a vampire at first did she?"

"That's none of your business." She hadn't and he'd been angry. None of that seemed to matter, now. "No one deserves to die like that."

"She didn't tell you, did she? And she bit you. Am I right?"

The tip of the pistol shifted from his temple to the spot on his neck that still ached from her bite. His anger at her betrayal paled in comparison to the desperation he was beginning to feel as the first rays of light bled over the horizon illuminating the morning clouds, blazing them mauve, magenta and orange. The bright orb of the sun had yet to make its appearance, but it was only a matter of minutes. Roger had to do something.

Julie stirred and tried to stretch. When her wrists

met resistance, her eyes opened and she stared straight into his. "Roger? What's happening?" Her voice sounded groggy as if she'd drugged.

"Chloroform is very effective on vampires. Did you know that?" Marley's voice was almost gloating. "She didn't even have a chance to put up a fight. Did you, my dear?"

"I'm going to kick your ass, Marley. I should have let Luke kill you. Instead I saved you and for what? So you could kill me? Fat chance." She struggled to free her hands, glancing over her shoulder at the horizon. "I'm going to kick your ass, Marley."

"Let her go." Roger knew it was only a matter of time before Parker climbed the stairs to the rooftop. But would he in time to save Julie? Roger couldn't wait to find out.

His hand jerked upward, knocking the pistol away from his neck, at the same time as he ducked and rolled away from Marley.

A shot rang out, hitting the roof beside Roger. "Don't move, or I'll kill you."

As the sun inched over the horizon, Julie still lay partially hidden from its killing rays in the shadows of an air conditioning unit. She didn't have much time and her hands weren't coming loose from the ropes Marley had used to bind her wrists. Still groggy from the chloroform, she couldn't seem to make her super-vampire strength work to free herself. "Let him go. It's me you want to kill, not him. Just let him go."

"No. I won't let him leave you here to die." Roger pushed to his feet and faced Marley. "Go ahead, shoot me, because I'm not going to let you kill her. I love her."

Julie's heart swelled as tears formed in her eyes. "No!" Julie fought her bonds. "Don't kill him. He's not a vampire. Roger, please, don't try to help me. Please don't die." Her tears tumbled down her cheeks.

He wasn't listening to her as he made his way across the rooftop.

Another shot rang out, hitting the tarpaper in front of Roger's feet. He kept walking, his gaze locked with hers.

"No, Roger. I don't want you to die," she cried, her shoulders shaking with her sobs.

He snorted. "And you think I want you to?"

"I mean it. I'll kill you." Bob Marley's voice wasn't nearly as convincing as he'd been before. "She has to die."

Julie's breath caught in her throat when another shot rang out.

Roger stopped only two feet from her and glanced over to Marley, a surprised look in his eyes.

Had he been hit? Julie's gaze scanned his body for the telltale sign of blood, but she didn't see any. Then a thump made her look to where Marley had been standing a

moment before. He lay at an odd angle on the rooftop, a bullet hole in his chest, his eyes open and staring at her. Behind him, at the door leading down into the apartment building, stood Chase Parker, Roger's partner.

Julie sagged against the clothesline, relief washing over her. At that moment the sun touched her leg, then her arm and the side of her face, her skin heating to a searing pain.

"Come on, we have to get you out of here." Roger pulled a knife from his pocket and hacked away at the ropes, blocking as much of the killing rays of the sun from her skin as his he could while he worked over her bonds.

In a few moments, he lifted her from the roof and ran toward the door just as the top of the building was bathed in sunlight.

Once the door was closed behind her, Roger set her on her feet and stared into her face. "Are you all right?"

"Yeah. I am now." Where the sun had burned her skin, the marks had already begun to fade. She shrugged and gave him a wry smile. "One of the perks. I heal fast."

"Come on, let's get you home." Without another word, he led the way down the steps to the bottom floor.

"I have a blanket in the trunk of my car. Wait here." Parker left them standing in the entryway and ran for the car.

When he returned, Roger wrapped her in the old wool army blanket and hustled her out to the Mustang, settling her low in the backseat.

Parker handed Roger the keys to his car. "Here, take my car. I'll handle everything here."

"You sure?" Roger stared hard at his friend and then stuck out his hand. "Thanks."

From her position in the backseat of the car, Julie called out, "Thanks, Chase. I owe you."

"Just get inside. I'll see you later. Maybe you can fill me in on everything then." Chase saluted her and pulled his cell phone from the leather case on his utility belt. "Go on."

Roger climbed in and shut the door. A moment later, the car roared to life and whipped out onto the street.

All the way to her place, Julie tried to think of something to say to him, but the longer Roger remained quiet, the less Julie wanted to break the silence. What was he thinking? Was he still angry at her? Did he wish he'd never met her? Did he really mean it when he'd said he loved her?

Julie bet he'd thought she was still unconscious when he'd said those three words. Perhaps she had been and she'd dreamed them.

The car finally eased to a stop and Roger leaped out. Once he'd adjusted the seat forward, Julie climbed from the back seat, the blanket wrapped around as much of her body as she could manage. She hurried into the old house, met in the entryway by William and Kim.

"Thank God." Kim wrapped her arms around her and hugged her close. "I thought he'd killed you."

"For a while there I thought he would too," Julie muttered into her friend's shirt.

"What about Marley?"

"He's dead." Roger stepped in and grabbed Julie's elbow. "If you have a moment, I'd like to talk."

Kim's eyes widened and she moved to stand next to William. "I'll be across the hall at William's, if you need me."

"I shouldn't, but thank you." Julie held her breath all the way up the stairs to her apartment, wondering what Roger could possibly have to say that he couldn't say in front of her friends. Or was this it and he was going to say he never wanted to see her again? Her feet slowed and she almost tripped. Why hurry to listen to that? It was the

last thing she wanted to hear from Roger's mouth. Could she just turn around and walk back out into the sun? Death by burning almost seemed preferable to dying of a broken heart.

Her feet continued moving and eventually she made it to her apartment and inside.

She stood with her back to Roger, listening to the sounds of him softly closing the door. Time to face the music.

Before she could take a deep breath, Roger's hands descended on her arms and he turned her to face him.

The haggard look on his face made her heart ache.

"I'm sorry, Roger. I should have told you," she blurted out.

"Shhh." He pressed finger to her lips.

"But I was wrong to keep it from you." She ducked her head, afraid to see the disappointment in his eyes. "You must hate me."

"Shut up." His words were followed by his lips, pressing against hers. The heat generated burned sweetly all the way down to her core.

"But—"

"I said shut up. I'm trying to kiss you."

Her eyes widened and her mouth opened slightly. "Oh."

Roger took advantage of her surprise and claimed her lips in a soul-defining assault, his tongue pushing past her teeth to tangle with hers.

When she came up for air, Julie's thoughts were jumbled and she fought to make sense of them. "I don't understand. I thought you hated me for lying to you."

"I never hated you. I was mad, but I never hated you." He kissed her again, his fingers cupping her chin. "How could I?"

She leaned her head against his chest, afraid to believe what she was hearing from the only man she'd ever loved. "I'm a vampire."

"So?"

"I can't go to the beach and lie in the sun?"

"Ever heard of walking along the shore in the

moonlight?" He blazed a trail of kisses down the side of her neck.

She gulped back the happiness his words gave her. "I can't have your children."

"Then I won't have to share you with anyone else." His fingers found the hem of her scrubs blouse and he lifted it up over her head. He unclasped her bra and slid the straps from her shoulders. He bent to take a nipple between his teeth, rolling it gently.

Julie's head dropped back, her breasts pushing out. "I'll outlive you."

He sucked the nipple into his mouth and let it go, making a loud popping sound. "I'll always love you."

"You're making it hard for me to let you go."

"Then don't." He tugged the elastic band of her scrubs bottoms downward.

When he reached the floor, she stepped free of her shoes and the pants, standing before him in her bikini panties, feeling incredibly sexy and loved. "Before we go any farther, I have one thing to say."

With his fists planted on his uniformed hips, Roger gave her a hard stare, the twinkle in his eyes softening the affect. "You've already told me you're a vampire. Are you keeping any other secrets from me that I should know?"

Julie melted from head to toe. He was the most handsome man she'd ever met, and she felt lucky that he loved her—a vampire. "I love you, Roger Decker."

He stood for a moment, his gaze narrow, his mouth pressed into a thin line. Then his lips turned upward and he grabbed her hand. "Good, now that we have that settled, come make love with me."

They ran for the bedroom laughing like a couple of teenagers in love, Roger stripping his uniform as he went.

When they lay beside each other on the bed, Roger asked, "Now, where were we?"

"About here, I think." She leaned up and kissed his lips.

"No, I think it was farther south."

She pressed him to his back and kissed his dark brown nipple. "How about here?"

"No. Lower."

Without wasting any more time, she got right down to business and took his cock full into her mouth. When she resurfaced, her lips poised at the tip, she smiled and asked, "Am I getting warmer?"

"Babe, you're fuckin' on fire." He dug his hands into her hair and pushed her down until he filled her mouth.

As her lips traveled up and down his length, she reveled in how thick and hard he was. He was just the right size to satisfy her and then some. Her hands closed around his balls, massaging them as she sucked his cock.

The hands in her hair pulled her off him. Then he flipped her onto her back. Lifting each leg, one at a time, he pushed them wide. He knelt between her thighs and pressed a finger to the mouth of her vagina. "So wet."

"You make me wet. Come inside me," she begged.

"Not yet." Dropping to his elbows, he settled between her legs and lifted her ass from the mattress, his tongue delving into her pussy. "Um, baby, you taste good."

"Fuck me, Roger. I'm on fire."

"Why are you in such a hurry?" Licking a path upward, he parted her thick folds and flicked his tongue over her clitoris.

With her heels dug into the mattress, she lifted up, wanting more. "Did I say I was in a hurry?" Her words came out in a breathless rush as waves of sensation tightened her muscles.

"You mean you have time for this?" He laved her pussy and clit, alternating between each.

"Oh yes!" She arched off the bed, pressing her cunt closer to his mouth, her fingers tangling in his hair, tugging him closer.

He sucked her clit into his mouth, flicking at the swollen nub until her entire body burst over the edge, shattering into million shards of glass, each a pinprick of fire inside.

When she fell back to the bed, he climbed up and over her, settling his cock against her pussy. There he paused, staring down into her face. "This morning, I almost lost you. I don't think I could bear to lose you."

"You seem to forget, I almost lost you too." She kissed the tip of his nose and reached up to cup his buttocks. "It's over. Now all I want is you inside me."

"That can be arranged." He pressed into her, stretching the walls of her channel in deliciously sensuous glide.

He'd come into her, like he'd come into her life, filling her heart with all the love he had to give and she'd love him with all her soul. For eternity.

TROUBLE WITH HARRY

TOMB RAIDER TROUBLE BOOK #1

Award Winning Author
Myla Jackson

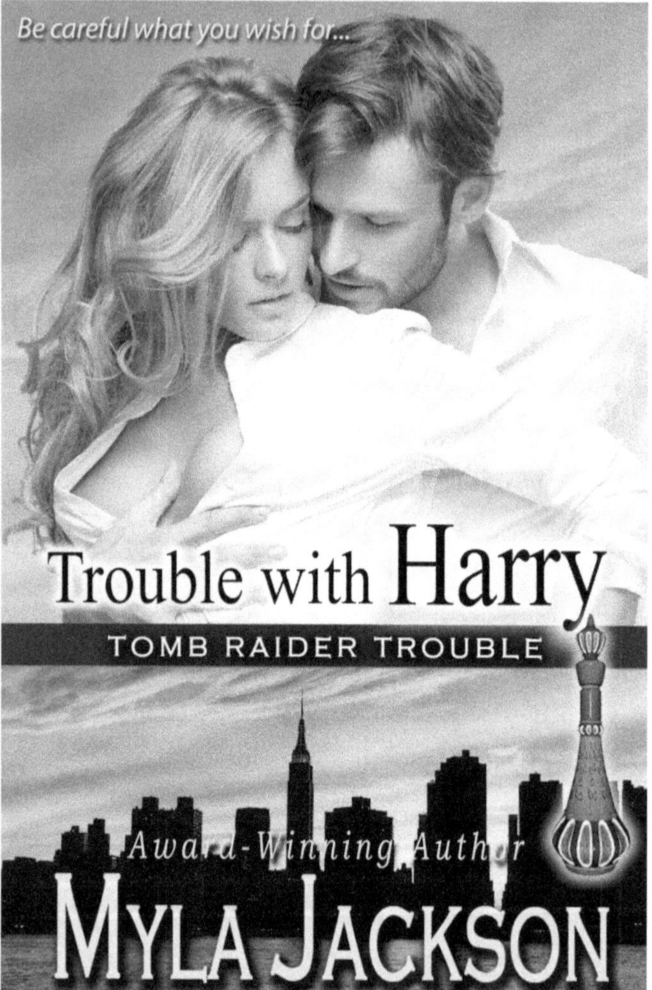

Be careful what you wish for...
Trouble with Harry
TOMB RAIDER TROUBLE
Award-Winning Author
MYLA JACKSON

Zagros Mountains in the Kingdom of Iraq 1924

H arry Taylor brushed his hat against his dust-crusted trousers and knelt in front of the sarcophagus. Pry bar in hand, he paused. Within the heavy coffin lay the culmination of five years searching, studying and digging in the driest of deserts near the base of the Zagros Mountains.

"Are you going to open it, or what?" William Prater, Harry's assistant and friend, stood on the other side of the stone platform, sand and sweat streaking his blond devil-may-care looks. "Whatever you do, hurry it up. You never know when those tomb guards will show again."

"Or the meddling British, for that matter. Give me a hand with this thing." Harry jammed the pry bar between the lid and the casing and leaned hard on it.

A crunching, scraping noise accompanied the incremental movement of the cover as it rasped across the top, revealing the treasure within.

A glint of light reflected off a shiny surface inside and a squiggly line of carved snakes appeared beneath Harry's arm. Adrenaline spiked in his system, sending blood racing to his heart. He'd done it! "William, my friend," he said in a reverent whisper, "we've found the tomb of Vashti, daughter of Azhi, the Devil Shah of ancient Persia."

"A princess, huh? She was probably daddy's little girl and completely spoiled. She better be loaded is all I got to say." Will leaned his shoulder into the lid and it slid to the side, where it teetered for a moment then fell with a resounding whomp, shaking the sandy floor of the tomb.

"I think we've hit pay dirt, Will." Harry straightened, tossing the pry bar to the ground, excitement bubbling up in his belly at what lay before him. A smile stretched his lips across his face, and he flipped his hat in the air. "Do you realize what we've found? Do you have any idea?"

Will stared down at the mummified remains of an ancient woman surrounded by decayed woven baskets and several unscathed decorative bottles. He frowned, his lips twisting in a lopsided grimace. "A mummy and some old bottles?"

Harry laughed, his voice echoing off the chamber walls. "Will, look past the dust and decay. Don't you see the details in the finely woven gown she's wearing? Look here, the embroidery is still intact. These symbols are those of the ancient lovers, Vis and Ramin. See the stone with the carving of a two-headed dragon lying over the mummy's head?"

"So, it just looks like a big dumb rock to me." Will shrugged. "Big deal."

"William, my man." Harry draped an arm around Will's shoulders. "Beneath that layer of dust is the most mystical stone known to man. Kings have fought wars to possess it, but it was lost long ago. Heinrich Schliemann himself couldn't find proof of its existence."

Will's chest puffed out. "But we did it, eh?" He gave Harry a skeptical glance. "So, why's it so damn important?"

"Because of the legend." Will's lack of enthusiasm irritated Harry. He began to wonder what Will thought he'd been searching for all these months. "The legends say that whomever touches the Stone of Azhi will have great powers. Powers to change the world as we know it. Powers to make every wish come true."

"My wish right now is for a ten-pound steak and a woman to share it with." Will licked his lips. "Suppose it might be worth something back in the States?"

"It's priceless—if only for its historical significance. But there are many men who would pay a king's ransom for its professed magical properties."

Will leaned over the mummy and reached for a dusty bottle. "I wonder what the bottles are for?"

"Probably contained the princess's favorite perfumes. Never mind them. It's the stone we want. No one's gonna pay for old glass when they can have all that power."

"Shit, I've been three long weeks without the comfort of a woman." Will waggled his eyebrows. "Does it have the power to grant me a woman?"

Harry was glad Will had finally understood the importance of their find. He slapped his friend on the shoulder. "Why settle for one? You could buy a dozen women with the money we'll make."

"Hell, I might even buy you one."

"No thanks." Harry lifted a bottle from the collection at the mummy's feet and brushed the dust from it. The blown glass reflected hues of deep sea green and blue, and was rimmed with gold bands.

"You aren't still mad about Fiona, are you?"

"Not in the least." He set the ornate container back in the sarcophagus.

Will lifted another of the glass bottles and tossed it lightly in the air, catching it one-handed. "Good, she's not your type anyway."

What was his type? Someone willing to follow him on wild chases across hostile continents? What woman in her right mind would do that? Harry didn't know and really wasn't too interested in finding out. Last one, Fiona, had tried to hem him in with ultimatums.

Had he stayed, he'd have resented her. Leaving her had been the only answer.

"I'm so hungry I could eat a steak the size of Cleveland about now." Will grabbed for the stone at the same time as Harry.

"Wait, Will. We need to be careful." What if the legends were true? Could the stone be dangerous? When his fingers felt the smooth points of the two-headed dragon, tingling spread from Harry's hand up his arm and into his chest. The tingling turned to a burning sensation.

"What the hell?" Will staggered backward, his forehead creasing into a frown. He stared down at his hands and shook them.

The floor trembled and the walls around Harry and Will shook. Dust rose and filled the air until Harry couldn't see the hand in front of his face, much less his friend. "Will!"

"Harry! What's happening?"

"I don't know." Harry's heart raced and his breathing came in short gasps, his lungs filling with sand. "I feel like I'm on fire."

"Let's get the hell out of here!" Will called out.

But the doorway remained shrouded in thick dust.

The burning intensified until Harry felt he'd been seared by the sun. He gagged and choked on the sand rasping against the lining of his throat. Giant stones fell from the walls and ceiling.

What a way to go. Just when he'd discovered the

stone of Azhi, he'd die in the mummified arms of the devil king's daughter.

The dim light from the torches snuffed out and blackness engulfed his tortured body. As if picked up by a tornado, he was jerked off his feet and sucked toward the sarcophagus, spiraling like a puff of smoke filtering through a tiny opening. His body screaming in pain, he could hear Will's terrified cries echoing his own. Then a loud thump ended the storm, sealing him in darkness. Harry drifted into oblivion, wondering what the hell had happened.

Twenty years of livin' and lovin' on a South Texas ranch raising horses, cattle, goats, ostriches and emus left an indelible impression on Myla Jackson, one she likes to instill in her red-hot stories. Myla pens wildly sexy, fun adventures of all genres including historical westerns, medieval tales, romantic suspense, contemporary romance and paranormal beasties of all shapes and sexy sizes. She lives in the tree-covered hills of Northwest Arkansas with her husband of more than 20 years and her muses—the human-wanna-be canines—Chewy and Sweetpea.

To learn more about Myla Jackson and her alter ego Elle James visit:

www.mylajackson.com
mylajackson@mylajackson.com

www.ingramcontent.com/pod-product-compliance
Lightning Source LLC
Chambersburg PA
CBHW070953120726
47910CB00004B/1212